Enough is Too Much Already

and other stories

JAN MARK

RED FOX

A Red Fox Book
Published by Random Century Children's Books
20 Vauxhall Bridge Road, London SW1V 2SA

A division of the Random Century Group

London Melbourne Sydney Auckland
Johannesburg and agencies throughout the world

'Enough is Too Much Already' first appeared in *Feet* (Kestrel Books, 1983),
'A Different Ball Game' in *A Sporting Chance* (Bodley Head, 1985), and
'Buzz-Words' in *A Quiver of Ghosts* (Bodley Head, 1987)

Bodley Head Original paperback published 1988
Red Fox edition 1991

Printed and bound in Great Britain
by Cox & Wyman Ltd, Reading, Berkshire

ISBN 0 09 985310 8

For Aidan Chambers

Contents

I

Enough is Too Much Already

'Look,' Maurice said, 'lay off, will you? I've told you I'm sorry, haven't I? I mean, I *mean* it. I *am* sorry.'

'You look it,' Nazzer said. 'You look so sorry my heart bleeds for you. Doesn't he look sorry?' said Nazzer, turning to Nina for confirmation. 'Tears pouring down his little face.'

'We waited outside for *half an hour*,' Nina said. 'It was freezing. Real brass monkeys. Cardy says she's not interested any more. We only *asked* her because you said you fancied her. Now she thinks I've been sending her up. Cardy's my best friend,' Nina said. 'Was.'

'If you'd been in my position,' Maurice began.

'Catch me in any position you'd be in,' said Nina. 'Next time you get your eye on a girl, you do your own fishing.'

'I'm not making excuses,' said Maurice. 'I've got a *reason*. I was unavoidably delayed. Nah, *shut* up, Nina, I'm trying to tell you. You know I nearly missed the train last night—'

'How should I know?'

'Because it was you kept me hanging about trying to set me up for Cardy—'

'I like that! You were the one—'

'I only suggested that she might like—'

'The way you go on anyone would think they were forming queues—'

'If you'll only listen,' Maurice said.

'I mean, you think you look so *glorious*—'

'Lady, give the guy a chance,' Nazzer pleaded. 'Turn down the goddam *volume*, willya?'

'Well I *did*.'

'What?'

'Nearly miss the train. It was about twenty-five past when I got to the station, and I'm just running on to the platform when old Patterson looms up like King Kong, out of a rubbish bin. I reckon he was trying to fish out the *Sun* while no one was looking. "Ho, Nicholls," he says, "didn't we have a little appointment at lunchtime?" and we had had, only I'd forgotten, and I said, "I can't stop now, Sir. I'll miss me train," and *he* started saying something, and the geezer on the public address started bawling something about a platform change, and would we all please pay attention, so I couldn't hear a word anyway—'

'*No*body can hear a word old Patterson says,' Nazzer remarked.

'—and old Patterson's still going on, so I just said, "Yes Sir, sorry Sir," and ran like hell and jumped on the train.'

'I heard,' Nina said. 'You don't have to tell me. It was on the News, this morning. *Maurice Nicholls caught his train. Norwich rocked to its foundations.* Right

10

before the earthquake in China, it was. And the Third World War breaking out.'

'Well, it looked all right, and I sat down, and got my physics out, like I was meant to have given Patterson at dinnertime, when this girl gets on.'

'I hope you don't think I'm going to tell Cardy all this?' Nina said. 'I mean, this is going to make her feel really marvellous, isn't it?'

'No, give it a rest,' Maurice said. 'I didn't really see her at first. I just noticed these legs going by.'

'Oh. Legs,' Nazzer murmured into his coffee. 'Legs.'

'*Not* what you think, Naz. You got a scaly mind. She was wearing those horrible wrinkly leg-warmers that look like lagging on old water pipes,' Maurice said.

'Thanks a million,' Nina said, peering under the table and adjusting something through her skirt.

'And anyway, she goes and stands up the front with all the other Red Berets—'

'Oh, a St Ursula's Virgin,' said Nazzer. 'Legs . . .'

'They *all* wear those short leg-warmers that only come up to your knees,' Nina said. 'It's some sort of fashion, or something. They *always* fall down.'

'—and she starts chatting to them, and then I see Langham up front, too.'

'Langham doesn't go on your train.'

'That's what I thought, and I'm just about to go up and say, "Get your great greasy body off our train, Langham," when he gets up for something, and she steps back and treads on his foot.'

'Yes?'

'What?'

'What happened?'

'Nothing happened,' Nazzer droned. 'You could drop a breeze-block on Langham's foot and he wouldn't notice. You could drop a breeze-block on his *head*—'

'He noticed, all right. He lets out this great horrible roar—you know, that sort of *Wrrroagh!* noise you get at First Division matches, and she turns round and says, "Oh, I'm sorry. Did I hurt you?" She had a nice voice,' Maurice reported, mournfully.

'And Langham starts mincing about and flapping his hands and squeaking, "Ooooh, Ai'm sorreigh. Did Ai hurt yaw?" and then the train starts—you know how those little pay trains jolt when they start—'

'They're only buses on rails,' Nazzer said. 'If they did away with the bridges they could have double-decker pay trains.'

'—and she falls against him, and he yells, "Oh, oh, she's after me, look, she fancies me, ooh-ooh-ooh!" and starts pulling her about, and she gives him a shove, and I can see him getting nasty—'

'*Getting?*' Nina said. 'He's a fat horrible pig, that Langham.'

'Well, I thought, someone'll stop it, but all the old geezers thought it was just kids mucking about, and let him get on with it. You know, she was really upset; you could see that, but they just went on reading the paper and looking out of the windows. I could just imagine them all sitting and watching a murder, like it was something on telly, and not doing anything about it.'

12

'What about the other Virgins?'

'Oh, I thought *they'd* do something, you know, I mean . . . there were *six* of them, but they just giggled a bit and looked the other way, and one of them said, "Some people'll do *anything* to get a bit of attention," and someone else says, "Oh, *her*," real snarky. And she tried to pull away from him but he got her by the strap of her bag—'

'This is getting really exciting,' said Nina. 'Isn't it, Naz? Don't you wish you could stay for the end?'

'It wasn't funny. You wouldn't have thought it was funny if it had been you. She had the strap wrapped round her wrist, and he kept twisting it—you know what a great lunk he is, Naz—'

'Why do people keep asking *me*?' said Nazzer.

'You pulled out of the Second Eleven because of Langham,' Maurice said. 'And this Cilla was only a small little thing.'

'Oh; *Cilla*, was it?'

'You know her?'

'No, but I mean—*Cilla*.'

''Sno dafter than Nina,' Nazzer said morosely, inspecting the bottom of his cup.

'I don't know how you've lived so long, Nazzer—'

'She was starting to cry, and the train was shaking around all over the points, and she nearly fell on me—'

'She seems to fall on a lot of people, this Cilla,' Nina remarked.

'So I got up and tapped Langham on the back of the neck—'

'Langham hasn't got a neck,' Nazzer said. 'His head grows out of his deltoids.'

'Watch your language,' Nina said.

'—with the edge of my physics book, and I said, "Lay off, Langham," and he looks at me and says, "You're going the long way home, aren't you?" I thought he was being cryptic, meaning, *I'm going to duff you up, shortly*, but I said, "Lay off, Langham, will you, or I shall have to rearrange you," and *he* said, "You and whose army?" '

'He would,' Nazzer said. 'I've never heard him come out with *anything* original; I don't reckon he *was* being cryptic, you know. He's not really programmed for it.'

'So I got my physics book and hit him behind the left knee.'

'Why the left knee?'

'He couldn't reach any higher,' Nazzer explained.

'The left knee is a vulnerable spot on Langham, right now,' Maurice said, 'since Saturday's match. You know what it's like, first match of the Autumn Term. There was a lot of old scores settled on Saturday; sort of backlog left over from Easter. Someone reckoned up with Langham's left leg. Anyway, it worked. He went over backwards, sort of Z-shaped. I wish you could have seen him, Naz. It would have made up for a lot.'

'I'll think about it in Maths,' Nazzer said. 'It'll cheer me up no end.'

'So I said to this girl, this Cilla, "Come on, let's get down the other end," and she said, "Supposing he follows us?" so I said, "I can always pull the emergency chain." '

'That's what Superman does, you know,' said

Nazzer. 'When Lois Lane's in peril, he flies to the rescue and pulls the emergency chain. And the emergency bog flushes,' he added.

'I was *joking*,' Maurice said, heavily. 'So anyway, we sort of stepped over Langham, and all these old geezers and ladies were sucking their false choppers, and old Langham was groaning, and this Cilla, she looks at me like I *was* Superman. I mean, it wasn't bad going, was it? I mean, it *was* Langham, and I did *thump* him.'

'What did the Virgins do?'

'Nothing. But they looked a bit envious,' Maurice conceded, modestly.

'He's not at school today,' Nina said.

'Maybe you killed him,' said Nazzer.

'Well, he *didn't* come after us, did he?' Maurice said. 'He couldn't. No, I didn't kill him. I saw him get off at Brundall. He was limping.'

'Brundall?'

'He lives at Brundall.'

'But you were on the Sheringham train.'

'Well, that's it, you see,' Maurice said. 'We weren't. We just arrived at the back end of the train, when we got to the place where the Sheringham line branches off, and I noticed we weren't on it. I mean, the track had branched off, but the train was still on the Yarmouth line.'

'So that's where you were,' Nina said. 'Yarmouth! I'm not telling Cardy. You'd better think of something better, or something.'

'No! It wasn't like that. See, I realized then that I'd got on the wrong train, so I thought, well, I'll get off at

Brundall, then I thought, no I won't, that's where Langham gets off— I'll get off at Buckenham. And so we got to Brundall and I see old Langham falling about on the platform—you *would* have enjoyed it, Naz—and then the conductor comes along, and I realized I'd only got my season to Worstead, and it's not even *on* that line, and this girl, this Cilla, she's still sitting next to me, sniffing, and I don't know where she's getting off, and I don't want to lose sight of her yet. So anyway, the conductor gets to us, and I say, politely, "You first," and she hums and hahs a bit, and the conductor says, "Where to, darling?" and in the end she says, "Reedham," and she blushes a bit, and says, "I don't really live there. I'm just going to see someone."

'He gives her a ticket.

'I say, "Can I come with you?" and she giggles and says, "Better not; it's my auntie."

'"And what about you?" says the conductor, to me.

'Well, I was stuck, wasn't I? I mean, we were just coming in to Buckenham, but I *couldn't* get off before she did. I didn't know her name or where she lived, or anything.'

'I thought you said her name was Cilla,' Nina snapped.

'Yes, but I didn't know that yet, did I? I had to find out, didn't I? And I ask you; Reedham! It's like the end of the world. And I said, "Berney Arms," because that's the next station after Reedham, and he says, "This train don't go to Berney Arms. This is the Lowestoft train."'

'I thought you said it was going to Yarmouth,' Nina said.

'It's the same line, till Reedham,' Maurice said. 'So I looked a right nutter, didn't I, and I said, "Oh, then I'll go on to Haddiscoe and borrow me brother-in-law's bike," so he gives me a ticket.'

'Your brother-in-law's out on the rigs, isn't he?' Nazzer said.

'His bike isn't.'

'No, his bike's in the garage down Earlham Road,' said Nina.

'The conductor didn't know that, did he?' Maurice said. 'Look, I was *lying*, for God's sake. I just wanted to find out a bit more about her. That's natural, isn't it?'

'If you say so.'

'I s'pose you'd forgot about us,' Nina said.

'Well . . . it was only ten to five, then. I hadn't even *started* thinking about you. So we got talking, and she says she's only just started at St Ursula's, and her name's Cilla Hales, and she lives in Wymondham, and I think that's brilliant, because the Wymondham train goes at five-twenty, so I can see her every evening, and then get the six o'clock home. Then we stop at Cantley, and all the other Virgins get out—what d'you think so many of them could be doing in Cantley? They can't all be Catholics out there—'

'There's nothing else to do,' Nazzer said, 'except the beet refinery, but that doesn't open till Monday.'

'Anyway, they all get out, and Cilla ducks her head down and says, "Stupid stuck-up cows," and then we talked a bit, and we're nearly at Reedham, and she's getting ready to go. So I say, "I'll see you tomorrow, shall I?" and she says, "Oh yes. Thanks ever so for—you know what," and I say, "Well, it was nothing. Let's meet in the buffet for coffee," and she says, "OK, let's," and then we're in Reedham.

'So, she got off, and waved at me from the platform as the train moved off. I hoped her auntie was meeting her, because the mist was coming down really thick. Oh God, it's like the end of the world, Reedham, it's like the end of the Universe.'

'End of the Universe's a time, not a place,' Nazzer said.

'Time and Place are the same thing,' Nina said. 'Old Patterson told us.'

'That's Time and *Space*.'

'It's right on the edge of the marshes—'

'What is?'

'Reedham.'

'I know,' Nazzer said. 'My mum took me there for a picnic when I was a young lad. I fell in a dyke and nearly drowned.'

'Are you sure they got you out in time?' Nina said. 'Brain death can occur after four minutes. I mean, you might have got left under for five.'

'Brain *damage*, not brain death,' Nazzer said. 'Brain death's when they pull the plug on your life-support system and break you up for spares.'

'—at least,' Maurice went on, 'I thought it was like the end of the world until we got to Haddiscoe. There's *nothing* at Haddiscoe, just two platforms. There's not even a bridge or a subway—you have to walk across the lines.'

'It's Doomsville, man.' Nazzer.

'Well, I got out of the train, I was the only one, and I stood and watched it going away into the mist—it was getting really thick by now, and I couldn't see anything, just the rear light on the train and a telephone box down the road. Well, I looked at the timetable and there's a train back from Lowestoft at thirty-three minutes past, so I ring me mum and say I won't be home for tea, and I go for a walk. In the mist. All on me tod.'

'Thinking about Cilla?' Nazzer played soulful music on an imaginary violin.

'Why not?' Maurice demanded. 'I'd done all right, hadn't I? And I was going to see her next day, so I thought it was worth getting stuck at Haddiscoe. I could hear this horrible noise, a sort of quiet tearing sound. It really frightened me, you know, it was all around. You couldn't see where it was coming from.'

'Don't think I've *ever* seen a noise,' Nina said.

'You ever been out in the garden at night and listened to the snails eating the lettuces? It was like that, only about a hundred times louder. Well, I walked around a bit, and went back to the station and waited, and the train didn't come and didn't come, and I thought they must have cancelled it. It was bloody cold, I can tell you, Naz—you'd never think it was only September.'

'We were cold too, weren't we, Naz?' Nina said.

'Anyway, it came in the end—I could hear it for ages before I could see it, and I got on.'

'What was the tearing noise?' Nazzer asked.

'Cows eating the grass,' Maurice said. 'They were

all over the place. I think they must go on eating all night, all the year round.

'Well, I sat on the train, and it was *crawling* along, because of the mist, and I was perishing cold, but I didn't really mind—I was thinking about Cilla. And then the train stopped at Reedham, and the door opened, and there she was.'

'Who?'

'Lois Lane,' said Nazzer.

'Cilla. Her. She came and sat down right opposite me and I thought, 'ere 'ere, and then she looked up and saw me. She went right pink—then green,' Maurice said.

'So I said, "That was a short visit, wasn't it?" and she said, "What happened to your brother-in-law's bike?" real snarky.

'And I said, "Wasn't your auntie in?" and she looked at me all funny and says, "Was your brother-in-law out?"

'And then she said, "You got straight back on the train, didn't you? You don't live round here at all, do you? Not even at Berney Arms," and I said, "No, well, actually I live at Worstead."

'She said, "Why were you going to Haddiscoe?"

'And I said, "I didn't want to get off the train before you did. I wanted to stay with you a bit longer," but it didn't work. She said, "But Worstead's on the other line," and I said, "I got on the wrong train." She said, "Well, why didn't you get off it?" and I said, "Like I said, I wanted to stay with you till you got out."

'And she said, "I was on the wrong train too. I only

got on to give my mate a book and that fat fella jumped on me."

'And I said, "Well, I saved you, didn't I?" and she said, "You might have said something. We could have got off at Brundall and hitched back."

'And I said, "You mean, you stayed on the train because of me?"

'And she said, "You mean, you only stayed on because of me?" and I said "Yes."

'And she said, "Blast you! I've missed the Wymondham train and there isn't another till half-past eight."

'And I said, "Well I can't get one till eight, either —that's nearly as bad. Let's have a coffee in the buffet at Norwich," and she said, "Bugger the buffet. My mum'll go spare when I get in," and she got up and went all the way to the other end of the train. I watched her, all the way.'

Nina said, 'Is that all?'

'*All?*' Maurice echoed. 'Isn't that *enough*?'

'Too much,' Nazzer murmured. 'Did you see her again?'

'In the distance,' Maurice said, 'and I saw her in the buffet at Norwich, but she wouldn't talk to me. When I sat down she got up and went to another table . . . So I followed her, and she got up and moved again, and I went over and said, "I don't know why you're so angry," and she said, "I suppose you think it's funny," and I said "Yes," and she said, "That's why I'm angry," and got up and found *another* table. She kept on doing it. It was like musical chairs. In the end I went out and got my train—and then I found I'd left my school bag with my season and all on Haddiscoe

Station. The cows have probably eaten it by now. My physics was in there too.

'Anyway, that's why I didn't come to the disco last night,' said Maurice.

2

A Different Ball Game

'Typical, isn't it?' Nina said. 'They did *Oliver* at Yarmouth. Stalham did *Bugsy Malone*, I mean, *Stalham*. What do *we* do? *The Mikado*.'

'You could plead pressure of work,' Nazzer said. 'All those re-sits.'

Maurice said, 'I don't know why *you're* complaining. You're just about the only one with a decent part. You haven't got to ponce around in the chorus with a fan.'

'Yes, I have,' Nina said. 'I've got to ponce around with a fan and *titter*. "Everything is a source of fun—nihihihihihihih." '

'But you're not a bloke,' Maurice said.

'Surprised you noticed,' said Nina.

'The staff have grabbed all the best parts, as usual,' Maurice said. 'Now they blackmail the rest of us into supporting roles because it's for famine relief.'

'I suppose you fancied yourself as the Mikado.'

'I wouldn't mind the Mikado,' Nazzer said. 'I like his style. "My object all sublime, I shall achieve in time, to let the punishment fit the crime . . ." '

'Fascist,' Maurice said.

'If the punishments fitted *your* crimes you'd have

been inside for the last five years,' Nina said. '"The idiot who in railway carriages scribbles on window panes . . ."'

'When I was a young lad and my mum used to send me upstairs for being bad, I used to breathe on the window and write HELP backwards in the steam, so it could be read from the street,' Nazzer said. 'I was dead thorough when I was seven.'

'Wore off then, didn't it? Who wrote BAN CRUISE on the bus and spelt it wrong?'

'C-r-u-i-s-e,' Nazzer said.

'Yes, but ban's only got one "n" in it.'

'I saw a good one in the gents at Caister,' Maurice said. 'Save energy—burn the rich.'

'I had this brilliant idea for a spy story,' Nina said. 'This woman, see, works for the Ministry of Defence, and writes classified information in the steam on her kitchen window and of course, it all fades off, and then her contact, who's got a job as her daily help and only turns up when she's out so they never meet, see, comes along and boils a kettle and the window steams over again and the words show up, and then *she* cleans the window, the contact, I mean, and destroys the evidence. It would work, wouldn't it? I mean, the Ministry suspect her and they bug her phone and search her flat and they've got the place under surveillance anyway, but they never see anything except this daily help cleaning the windows, dead natural.'

Nazzer said, 'Why don't they just write letters to each other? Anyway, what does he do to people who scribble on window panes?'

'Who?'

'The Mikado.'

'I can't remember,' Maurice said. 'I like the bit about the billiard sharp: ". . . and there he plays extravagant matches, in fitless finger-stalls, on a cloth untrue, with a twisted cue and elliptical billiard balls—" '

'Colleoni, him with the monument in Venice, had three of them,' Nazzer said.

'Three what?'

'Balls. Not many people know that,' said Nazzer.

'I shouldn't think many people want to,' Nina said.

'I tried it once,' Nazzer remarked. 'I wonder what they put in this coffee.'

'I don't think they put anything *in*,' Maurice said. 'I think it's made from what they take out of ordinary coffee to make it pure.'

'Tried what?'

'What?'

'What did you try once?'

'Playing billiards with elliptical balls—well, it was snooker, actually.'

'Sounds like Rugby,' Nina said. 'What did you do, pick up the ball and run round the table with it?'

'No, it was two Yanks I met on the Ludham bus. I must have told you.'

'Perhaps it was in the Old Days, before we knew you,' Maurice said.

'Hard to believe, isn't it?' Nina said. 'There was a time when we didn't know him. He always seems to have been there, like Maggie Thatcher.'

'I was still at the High School, anyway. We had that daft blazer badge with five gold rings and a monogram no one could read. It was the badge that did it.'

'Did what?'

'Well, that helped, but it was really the eggs.'

'Oh,' Nina said. 'Oh—oh. Not your auntie again.'

'You didn't mind borrowing her post-hole borer that time,' Nazzer said. 'No, this was when she *first* started with the chickens. They all went broody at once.'

'Sort of collective hysteria,' Maurice suggested.

'Something like that. Well, it was dead embarrassing because she was just getting orders from all these free-range freaks from London, you know, the ones on the high-fibre kick at weekends and cholesterolburgers Monday to Friday—'

'I thought eggs *gave* you cholesterol—'

'Everything gives you cholesterol,' Maurice said. 'Even things that used to make you go blind, now they give you cholesterol.'

'*Anyway*,' Nazzer said, 'she rang up Mum for advice and Mum said she could borrow her china ones.'

'China chickens? They'd take a hell of a time to cook.'

'China eggs,' Nazzer said. 'She sends me over to Ludham on the bus with all these eggs in a paper bag. Twenty-five eggs and it was raining like the clappers. I was soaked by the time the bus came. Well, I put the bag on the seat to dry out, but it was wetter than I thought. After a bit Nature took its course—'

'You mean they *hatched*?' Maurice said.

'No, the bag disintegrated. Well, I didn't notice. I was watching this girl up at the front.'

'You would of been,' Nina said. 'I bet that's why

26

you failed Eng. Lit. You were sitting behind Lisa Pestell.'

'She's got lovely action,' Maurice said, 'even when she's writing.'

'I mean, *Eng. Lit.* You can talk about re-sits,' Nina said, bitterly.

'*Anyway*, like I said, I didn't notice the bag till I heard this clucking across the gangway, so I looked round and there were these two blokes stretching their necks and making with the elbows like Kentucky Fried Chicken. I didn't think anything of it, at first, I mean, I thought they were eyeing this girl too and it was a sort of foreign mating call—'

'How did you know they were foreign?'

'By the accent. You wouldn't think you could cluck in a Yank accent, would you, I mean, you wouldn't think it would *show*; anyway, then I saw they were looking at me, and grinning, so I sort of glanced down, casually, like I'd been meaning to glance down anyway, and I saw this damp rag that had been the bag, and all the eggs sort of nestling round my bum.

'So one of these blokes goes, "Did you lay them all at once?" and the other one goes, "He never laid all those himself. He's just hatching them for a friend," and he clucked, and the other one crowed, and I thought, 'Ere 'ere, this could go on all the way to Ludham, so I said, "You didn't think they were eggs, did you?" and they went a bit quiet because, I mean, they were *obviously* eggs, but I didn't think they'd know what they were made of. I said, "Don't you know blanks when you see them?"'

'And the little thin one goes, "Blanks? They're

27

blanks? My god, what do you fire them from, a bazooka?" So I said, "Not that sort of blank, these are snooker blanks," and the other one said, "You play snooker with *eggs*?"

'Why didn't you just say they *were* eggs?' Nina asked. 'I mean, why all this with the snooker?'

'Because it was just after Dad got the snooker table. I was sort of inspired. Anyway, I wasn't going to have those two clucking at me till we got to Ludham. So the first one said, "I suppose it's an English version, is it?" and I hadn't thought of that. Then I realized he was being serious and he wouldn't know anyway, I mean, games are different abroad—look at American Football, so I said, "Oh, this is Real Snooker."

'His friend goes, "Real as opposed to what?" and I said, "You've heard of Real Tennis?"

'"Oh, Court Tennis, the ancient kind," says the big one—I loved the way he said ancient, like it was something they didn't have, I mean, he seemed pleased he knew the right word, so I said, "Well, it used to be Royal Tennis, like Real Madrid," but they hadn't heard of Real Madrid. I think they thought it was another ball game.'

'You could say that,' Maurice said.

'The first one says, "I've never heard of it," and I said, "Oh, it's not played much outside the Public Schools," and the thin one says, "Oh, you're a Public School man, what?" I don't know what he'd been reading. He put on this English accent. It wasn't bad—I mean, you could tell it was meant to be English.'

'They can't do Cockney, though, can they,'

Maurice said. 'Remember *Mary Poppins*?'

'Marlon Brando did it in *Mutiny on the Bounty*,' Nina said.

'That wasn't Cockney, though, was it. Anyway, the new version's better.'

'Well, I said yes, and the little one says, "Eton or Harrow?" so I said, "No, Scunthorpe, actually," and showed them the badge.'

'*Scunthorpe*,' Maurice said.

'Well, if you don't know Scunthorpe it doesn't sound that daft. Specially if you come from Detroit or somewhere like that.'

'I dunno,' Nina said. 'Detroit might be just like Scunthorpe.'

'Did they?'

'What?'

'Come from Detroit?'

'No, Tottenham, Ohio.'

'I've got a cousin in Scunthorpe,' Nina said. 'The name means someone with a squint used to live there in Danish.'

'I expect that's why he lived there,' Maurice said. 'He probably thought he was somewhere else.'

'How d'you con anyone into thinking you went to Public School?' Nina demanded.

'He does talk more snobby than us.'

'That's only because I come from Dagenham,' Nazzer said. 'Anyway, I've got this aristocratic profile.'

'You've got a long hooter.'

'Well, I told them that Scunthorpe was founded in the nineteenth century to provide a classical education

29

for the sons of provincial gentlemen and that the game of Real Snooker originated there. They used to use live ones, I said. Eggs, that is.'

'They never swallowed that?'

'Why not? I read somewhere that snooker started in an Officers' Mess. It used to be very up-market, snooker. Then it went down-market.'

'Where is it now?'

'Just marketable. Well, one of them says how does it differ from regular snooker? So I said it required a lot more skill as you couldn't easily tell which way an oblate spheroid would roll—'

'A *what*?'

'An oblate spheroid. Like the earth. If you had the earth on a table and poked it with a snooker cue it might go *any* way unless you knew where to poke it.'

'Haven't I heard that somewhere before?' Maurice said.

'Archimedes. "Give me but one firm spot on which to stand—and a long enough cue—and I will move the earth." Archimedes said that.'

'I thought he said Eureka.'

'That was afterwards,' Maurice said. 'It rolled off the table.'

'Anyway, they said, where could they get a game? I should have sent them to Scunthorpe—I don't suppose I'd ever have seen them again, but like an idiot I said we had this table at home. Well, we did. Just. Anyway, we got talking and they said, any chance they could come and play? and I said yes, sure, but I'd have to get the blanks balanced first as they were new.'

'Balanced?'

'I was stalling. I mean, I had to give these eggs to my auntie, hadn't I, what with her hens lined up screaming for them.'

'You could have given them a false address, couldn't you?' Nina said, 'like that time the Mormons got you in the Haymarket and wanted to come round and do a conversion job.'

'I still feel bad about that,' Nazzer said.

'Where d'you send them?' Maurice said.

'Next door but three—the Rathbones,' Nazzer said. 'They're Jehovah's Witnesses. No, but I wanted to see what would happen.'

'What did happen?'

'There was a big confrontation in the porch—and half-way down the path. I watched out of the landing window but I couldn't tell if they were converting each other or beating each others' heads in. Gentle Jesus meek and mild wasn't in it,' Nazzer said. 'Gentle Jesus, ladies and gentlemen, was *nowhere*.'

'Church militant,' Maurice said.

'No, I mean, what happened with the eggs?'

'Well, I had to give them to my auntie, didn't I? But all the way back in the bus I was working out the rules. I thought, I mean, suppose you played the whole thing with eggs, it would be chaos, but, I thought, suppose you used eggs instead of the reds and used a red for a cue ball, it would be quite interesting and anyway, if you used *all* eggs you'd have to dye most of them. When I got in I asked Mum if she had any more and she said why, and I said that I'd been doing a bit of thinking on the bus—well, I had, hadn't I?' Nazzer said, aggrieved, '—because it had struck me that they were just what I needed for school. This experiment in physics—'

'Which experiment's that?'

'Oh, I made it up. Something about Newton's Fourth Law of Motion.'

'There's only three laws of motion.'

'Not any more,' said Nazzer. 'There's Pollard's Law of Motion as well, now. And she said she had another nine so after tea, when she'd gone out, I had a go.'

'Your old man had something to say about that, didn't he?'

'He was in Manchester that week. Just as well; he'd have put on his parts if he'd seen me anywhere near that table. Well, you know, it was fascinating, those eggs. If you hit them near the blunt end they rolled round in a sort of semicircle sometimes, but usually they went up on end and *twirled*. And if you hit them end on, they stalled—that looked really clever. And then I saw that it wasn't so daft after all, because if you got them dead in the right spot they rolled just like an ordinary ball, I mean, there was a lot of skill in it. After an hour I was a lot better at hitting eggs than I was when I started.'

'Yes,' Maurice said, 'but what about the cue ball?'

'Ah, that was it. I had to decide: did I use an egg for a cue ball, or did I make a triangle with nine—'

'You couldn't make a triangle with nine,' Maurice said, 'no way.'

'Yes, well, it wasn't a triangle it was a rhombus, but it would have been where the triangle should be—*or*,' Nazzer said, 'did I dye six of them and use them as coloureds? Well, I decided to keep them in the middle.

I mean, an egg as a cue ball was *fiendish*. I suppose if you kept at it long enough you'd get really brilliant at hitting it in the right place, it would really be an achievement, but there wouldn't be any fun in it. You couldn't play badly and have a bit of a laugh. You couldn't play *fairly* well and just get by. Either you'd have to be World Class or you couldn't play at all. It wasn't like chess.'

'It wouldn't be,' Nina said. 'Not with eggs.'

'But then I found it was just as hard to pocket an egg with the cue ball. I mean, that really was Grand Master stuff. You'd have to be one of the all-time greats to do it more than about once in a hundred shots. So I thought perhaps I'd better use them as coloureds so we'd only have six of them to cope with. Only that meant dyeing them.'

'Weren't you taking all this a bit seriously?' Maurice said. 'I mean, it was only a game. Well, it wasn't even that, really.'

'There was the honour of the school at stake,' Nazzer said. '*Floreat* Scunthorpe and all that. Anyway, what about hospitality to foreigners? The English have got a lousy track record on that. I'd asked these blokes over to play Real Snooker and by God they were going to play Real Snooker, even if I had to invent it.'

'You did have to invent it.'

'I call that really conscientious,' Nina said.

'Then I thought, Mum'll go really spare if I spoil all her eggs. Suppose she needed them again some day? It might cause grave alienation among the chickens if you gave them blue and green eggs.'

'Aren't birds colour-blind?' Nina said.

'I don't think so,' said Maurice. 'I mean, why would the males get themselves up in all those feathers if the she-birds couldn't see the colours?'

'Same reason you put pink streaks in your hair, I suppose,' Nina said. 'Nobody notices.'

'Still, I thought I'd see how it looked so I went into the kitchen and got out the cochineal.'

'What's cochineal?' Maurice said.

'It's that red food-colouring,' Nina said. 'They make it out of beetles.'

'Oh, yes, beetlejuice,' Nazzer said. 'Named after the large red star in the constellation of Orion.'

'I thought that was shellac,' Maurice said.

'There's no star named Shellac,' Nazzer said.

'*No*. Shellac's made with beetles.'

'It's probably a different kind of beetle,' Nazzer said. 'Think of all those innocent insects sacrificed to make one bottle of food-colouring. I wonder if vegetarians know that.'

'Do vegetarians mind eating insects?' Maurice said.

'I don't suppose they get the chance all that often. Anyway, the egg came out horrible—all streaks,' said Nazzer. 'Then I remembered that it was *Real* Snooker. There was nothing in the rules—'

'What rules?'

'*My* rules. Nothing to say where the colours ought to go so I laid out the table with eight whites—blanks —eggs—in the middle—'

'I thought you said there were nine.'

'One was all over pink streaks, wasn't it? There was no way I could pretend it was *meant* to look like that. Then I put out six reds where the colours should be and

34

used the black for a cue ball. It looked funny,' Nazzer said, 'but quite convincing. I spent the rest of the evening practising. I got quite good at it—I even potted a couple.'

'I thought that was Aldebaran,' Nina said.

'*What?*'

'The big red star in Orion.'

'Well, Mum gave me a funny look next day when she came upstairs. She goes, "There's two fellows downstairs called Tom and Randy saying they've come for the Real Snooker. There's none on the box," she says.'

'Aldebaran's in Taurus,' Maurice said.

'Funny how Americans go round calling themselves Randy,' Nina said. 'You think someone would tell them.'

'They gave me a funny look, too, when they saw the house. I suppose they thought someone from Scunthorpe School would live in a mansion, but I let on that my parents had made great sacrifices to send me to a good school. I just hoped Mum wouldn't come in because she says that Scunthorpe's the one town in England that turns out to be just like you thought it would. I didn't tell them that all the sacrifices had been to buy the snooker table. This was before we built the extension—you could just get round the table if you wore very tight trousers.

'Well, I showed them the rules—'

'I thought you'd made them up?'

'Yes, but I'd typed them on Dad's portable. I explained that this kind of thing didn't really get written down much—in the Public Schools, you

35

know. Chaps just passed them on by word of mouth.'

'Oh, *chaps*.'

'I don't think they have blokes in Public Schools,' Nazzer said. 'Any more than we have chaps in ours.'

'Didn't Prince Charles call people blokes, once?' Maurice asked.

'Yes, but he was talking about the working classes,' Nazzer said. 'I mean, *he's* a chap, isn't he?

'Well, we had coffee and talked a bit—I mean, really, they were all right. If I hadn't been lying to them I'd have quite liked to make friends but it did take the edge off it a bit—lying,' Nazzer said. 'I suppose I'm just basically very honest. But they didn't much want to talk, they wanted to start playing. Well, I was OK, I mean, I *knew* how to play. I hadn't done anything else for twenty-four hours, hardly, so I let Tom tee-off—'

'That's golf.'

'*And* Real Snooker—well, it was only breaking the Triangle.'

'Rhombus.'

'It wasn't even that now. It was an irregular pentagon only I called it the Oval because of the eggs and Tom teed-off, and the eggs went all over the shop, and so then I had first shot. It was magic. I potted an egg—a blank. Well, that didn't happen again. It was just as well, really, because then they had to try it and they saw how brilliant I must be. There were eggs going every which way. Tom didn't like it much. He said, "This is crazy. Call this a game? No wonder you conquered half the known world." Either he was quoting somebody,' Nazzer said, 'or I was getting right up his nose. But Randy really got stuck in. Tom said he was a pool shark; he looked like some kind of a shark anyway. I've never seen jaws like it—wall-to-wall teeth.'

'They have orthodontists,' Maurice said. 'They don't go to the dentist.'

'I reckon Randy went to a monumental mason. Anyway, he got really fanatical about it. Me and Tom left him to it and went into the other room to play poker, but every time we called in to see how he was doing, he was improving. I mean, after a couple of hours he was actually potting eggs—blanks. Then he got clever and starting using an egg for a cue ball, you know, what I'd thought was impossible. Then he challenged me to a frame. It went on for an hour and ten minutes—one frame, but he won. It was dead embarrassing.'

'I'd like to have seen that,' Nina said. 'You embarrassed. Sort of once-in-a-lifetime experience, like Halley's Comet.'

'Well, anyway, it was getting late. They went before Mum came back, though, and Randy took the rules—and an egg to practise with. He said he didn't see why he shouldn't introduce New World variations.'

'You mean, they never did suss you?'

'Why should they? It wasn't just because they were Yanks—there must be a lot of people in London have never seen a china egg.'

'Or Scunthorpe,' Nina muttered.

'Where my sister's teaching she says there's kids from centrally heated flats who'd never seen coal.

They'd heard of it but they didn't know what it looked like. I mean, if you went to America and someone started a volleyball game with a melon and said it was an old Cherokee custom or something, you wouldn't know any different. Didn't they used to play lacrosse with snowshoes?'

'People used to play soccer with a bladder,' Nina said. 'I read that somewhere.'

'Association Footbladder doesn't sound right,' Maurice said. 'Spot the Bladder competitions; no . . .'

'Yes,' Nazzer said, 'but what bothers me is, suppose there's enough maniacs like Randy in Tottenham, Ohio, it might catch on. It might be catching on already. It might get really big. I mean, we've got championship darts already, on telly, and Olympic synchronized swimming. Suppose we got International Real Snooker? Can't you imagine it? Late-night coverage by satellite from Madison Square Garden; Real Snooker stars running chat shows; Real Snooker stars buying night clubs; Real Snooker stars throwing tantrums and bashing the ref over the head with a cue rest. And people coming round to interview Anthony "Nazzer" Pollard, the obscure Norfolk schoolboy who gave the game to the world. Suppose they try to find Scunthorpe School?'

'I shouldn't worry,' Maurice said. 'Tell them you meant Scunthorpe, Massachusetts.'

'Is there one?'

'If there isn't one you can invent it. After all,' Maurice leered at him, 'that's what you're good at.'

'Tell you what,' Nina said, 'we've missed the rehearsal.'

3

Buzz-Words

'Why shouldn't bees have souls?' Maurice said.

'What do they want souls for?' Nina asked. 'They don't go to church.'

'There was that wasps' nest over the altar at St Anselm's Without.'

'They weren't there to worship,' Nazzer said. 'They didn't know it was a silly place to park until the men from the council moved in.'

'Well, you get these nutters that think animals go to heaven. They have pet cemeteries with little crosses: *In Memory of Dear Rover. United with Gran.*'

'The nutters who worry me are the ones who think *they're* going to heaven.'

'What about worms? There aren't going to be worms in heaven. What about tsetse flies?'

'Worms don't have souls,' Nazzer said. 'They don't even have brains. They have ganglia. If you mince up an educated worm and feed it to an ignorant one, the ignorant worm gets clever.'

'How do you test a worm's IQ?' Nina said. 'My sister had a ganglion, on the side of her little toe. She hit it with a book and it disappeared. That's standard practice for ganglions.'

'You get much the same effect with worms, I dare say,' Nazzer remarked, 'if you hit them with a book.'

'They'll have to keep the numbers down somehow.'

'Where?'

'In heaven. There's more insects in one English garden than there are Chinese.'

'There's no Chinese in our garden,' Nina said. 'Anyway, there's no point in animals having souls. They don't have a sense of sin.'

'Dogs have a sense of sin,' Maurice said.

'They have a sense of guilt,' Nazzer said. 'Most of them look guilty all the time, even when they haven't done anything, except for those mongrels that grin and run sideways.'

'OK,' Nina said, 'there'll be dogs in heaven, but they've got to draw the line somewhere. They'll have a sort of interviewing room, like down the social security, with a counter, and St Peter asking test questions, you know: "Well, Tiddles, are you sorry you ate the budgie?"'

'That wouldn't work,' Nazzer said. 'Tiddles will say, "No, I am not sorry I ate the budgie because that is what budgies are for and anyway, I already got booted for eating the budgie, also for making a nest in the shredded wheat. You're not going to send me down for that, are you, Guv?"'

'Tiddles will go to Limbo,' Maurice said. 'A sort of Butlins for cats and atheists.'

'I think it'll be like Customs,' Nina said. 'People with nothing on their consciences will go through the green channel, like Tiddles and his budgie—nothing to declare.'

40

'What about the budgie?' Nazzer said. 'Where's that going?'

'That wouldn't work either,' Maurice said. 'Think of all the villains and loonies with nothing on their consciences. Hitler would go through the green channel.'

'They'll be on the lookout for Hitler,' Nazzer said. 'They'll have something more foolproof than the green channel.'

'Well, they've got God, haven't they? He'll do the real sorting out.'

'God delegates,' Maurice said. 'That's what he's good at. Don't forget the middle management.'

'Clergymen?'

'I was thinking of angels.'

'Angels sit on the Board and have executive lunches. They make policy decisions. Bishops are more area supervisors.'

'That's only for people; there's got to be someone looking out for the non-human clients. You know, East Midlands Superintendent of Dogs, Goats and Large Rodents.'

'What about the bees?'

'The bees are going to Butlins, aren't they? With the atheists.'

'I think you've got it wrong about atheists. It's pagans who get off with a caution. I should think atheists will be interned.'

'Like I said, Butlins. Atheists won't be expecting heaven, anyway, will they? They'll just expect to be dead.'

'Bees won't be expecting heaven, either,' Nina said.

'I mean, that's what we were saying, isn't it? They just spend their lives being bees. They don't try to be *better* bees.'

'That's the trouble with evolution,' Nazzer said. 'There's no incentive to try harder, no productivity bonus. Natural selection does it for you.'

'What about reincarnation?' Maurice said. 'That's an incentive, if you like. If you don't do well enough the first time round you come back as a bee.'

'That would solve the overcrowding problem,' Nina said. 'All the atheists will have to start over as bees and work up through rats and goats until they get human status again. That way you just end up with people.'

'Not necessarily,' Maurice said. 'For all we know bees are at the top of the list. We may be bad bees, working our way up to being bees again. People may be the bottom rung of the ladder. Bees may turn out to be the highest form of life, soul-wise.'

'If they've got souls.'

'I mean, they do better than most people, most of the time, don't they? Well organized, stable economy—'

'One party politics.'

'And moral. They're much more moral than we are. They sting each other to death.'

'Your average bee,' Nazzer said, 'is not particularly intelligent.'

'I never said it was. I said bees are well organized.'

'Someone's got to do the organizing,' Nina said. 'Stands to reason, there's got to be one intelligent bee calling the shots.'

'Bees have a corporate mentality,' Maurice said.

'Like Japanese office workers,' Nina said. 'They all stand up in the morning and sing the Company song.'

'I suppose it's a kind of collective subconscious, isn't it?' Maurice said. 'No one gives the orders, they just know what to do instinctively, so they do it.'

'Programmed,' Nina said. 'I mean, don't you need a brain, for instinct? Bees don't have brains, do they, Naz? Any more than worms.'

'I don't think anyone's ever run an encephalograph on a bee,' Nazzer said.

'They must have some sort of a brain,' Maurice said. 'Even fleas have brains, they must have. How else do they learn to do tricks? Bees are bigger than fleas.'

'Bison are bigger than people,' Nazzer observed. 'Come to that, bison are bigger than fleas. A bison-sized flea could do a lot of damage; a kind of intercontinental ballistic bison. How far would it be able to jump, Maurice?'

'Wouldn't work,' Maurice said. 'The skeleton would collapse under the weight.'

'Fleas are exoskeletal,' Nazzer said. 'It's a different principle entirely.'

'It doesn't make any difference whether you wear your bones on the outside or the inside,' Maurice said. 'They still have to carry your weight. Gravity's always a problem. If you dropped a flea down a deep hole it wouldn't notice. A bison would burst.'

'What about cats, then?' Nina said. 'Cats are smaller than dogs, but they're a sight brighter. You never get a cat letting anyone teach it tricks. Ever seen a performing cat?'

'It's got nothing to do with the size,' Maurice said. 'It's brain area. Better to have a small wrinkled surface than a large smooth one.'

'You should know,' Nina said.

'Walnuts are more intelligent than almonds,' Nazzer said; 'it's a well-known fact.'

'It still wouldn't mean they've got souls.'

'Walnuts?'

'Bees.'

'There was a film once: *The Spirit of the Hive*.'

'That was foreign.'

'They've got ghosts,' Maurice said.

'Phantom bees?'

'No, that's what I meant by corporate mentality; not individual bees, a whole swarm.'

'Why not phantom bats?' Nina said, meaningly, 'in the belfry?'

'I don't know about bats,' Maurice said, 'but look at that.'

'Your arm? I've seen that before, somewhere,' Nina said.

'And what's that on my arm?'

'Hairs,' Nazzer said. 'And a pimple. And that scar where Jaggers tried to saw you in half with a ruler. Are you going to put it on exhibition? I'll write you a guide book if you cut me in on the takings.'

'Drop the wisecracks,' Maurice said. 'What are *these*?'

'Flea bites,' Nina said. 'Who've you been snogging with, Anna Witchard? Don't you know about the Witchards?'

'That's nits,' Nazzer said. 'All the nits in North

Norfolk come from the Witchards. Every time they move there's a new outbreak.'

'These are not nit bites, they're bee stings,' Maurice said. 'And look here, on my neck.'

'Never knew Anna Witchard had such sharp teeth.'

'Nits.'

'Don't you know a bee sting when you see one? There's two more on my back, lower down.'

'I don't think we want to see them, thanks all the same,' Nina said.

'Bee stings in February?' Nazzer said. 'Pull the other one.'

'If I had nits I wouldn't advertise them in the canteen,' Nina said.

'It'll be a special species of winter bee,' Nazzer said, 'imported from the Soviet Union. They have extra long fur and leather wings. There used to be quite a trade in beeskin coats until the Hymenoptera Liberation Front moved in.'

'Get lost,' Maurice said. 'These were the usual sort of bee, only they died last week and they stung me on Saturday.'

'Like my grandad,' Nina said. 'Gran last saw him six months after he died.'

'Did he sting her?' Nazzer asked.

'No, he was standing on the bend in the stairs. It was during a power cut and she was just going up to bed with a candle when she saw him there. She said afterwards that she didn't think much about it at first because he always did spend a lot of time just standing about, and then she remembered he was dead, so she went back down again for another look. He was still there. He said, "Hello, Edith," and she said, "Hello, Arnold," and he said, "I've just come back to see how you're getting on," and she said, "I'm all right, thank you, Arnold," and he said, "Well, I'll be going, then," and he stood around for a bit longer and then he sort of went frilly at the edges and disappeared. Mum was furious with her when she told us. She thought Gran ought to have asked him where he'd come back *from* and what it was like. Gran said, "Well, he never did have much to say for himself, did he?" '

'I expect she imagined it,' Nazzer said. 'Like you said, she was used to seeing him standing around.'

'Yes, but she said it was exactly like him.'

'Of course it was. That's *just* how she would have imagined him. If this goat, say, had turned up on the stairs with horns and yellow eyes and said, "Hello, I am Arnold, back from the grave," that *would* have been convincing.'

'Did she have any proof?' Maurice said.

'What sort of proof?'

'Supernatural marks; like my bee stings?'

'Supernatural nits.'

'Look, forget the nits. These are bee stings and I got them on Saturday when I went over to Hickling.'

'I meant to ask you about that,' Nina said. 'You were supposed to be helping with the coffee morning.'

'I rang up,' Maurice said. 'I rang twice, but there was no one in. Where were you?'

'*I* was at the coffee morning,' Nina said.

'I was digging out tree stumps, in this weather, I ask you. You know what it was like on Saturday,' Maurice said. 'I went out expecting pneumonia and what do I get? Bee stings.'

'So you keep saying. I think this is just a cover-up for some horrible disease you've got and there's no known cure,' Nazzer said. 'They're just buboes.'

'They are not buboes. Listen, you know my uncle does landscape gardening? Well, he had this big job on over the weekend and his partner was off sick—'

'Told you,' Nazzer said. 'I suppose he'd come out in lumps, too.'

'Yes, he had. Look, if you'll just listen; my Uncle Dave rang up on Friday night and said that Joe—that's his partner—had been taken ill at work and could I come over and help? Well, I don't know what had happened, neither did he, so I said I'd go.

'I hitched a lift over to Hickling—*after* I'd tried to ring you, Nina, and there's Dave in the kitchen with Joe's wife, and she's carrying on about Joe being delirious and covered in stings. Only we didn't know about it being stings, then, and she always does go over the top. Every little earache's meningitis. She said he'd come home from work all swelled up and moaning about buzzing in his head, but he couldn't see anything. I thought she meant that his eyes were so swelled he couldn't see anything.'

'They do a lot of swelling up over that way, don't they,' Nina said. 'I don't know that I go for all this with the stings. It could be some sort of lurgy that no one knows anything about.'

'Like I said,' Nazzer muttered, 'a plague, unknown to science. Millions will perish.'

'Only if they go to Hickling first,' Maurice said. 'Dave was worried in case it was some sort of pesticide and Joe was reacting to it. *They* never use it; he's very organic, Dave is; chews his compost up with his own teeth, sort of thing, but you never know what people have been putting on the land, out there. Anyway, Joe's wife swore he'd been stung and the doctor said that's what it looked like, so we got in the Land Rover and went over to see.'

'The swellings?'

'No, the site; Tokesby Holmes Farm. You know how much rain there's been lately; it looked like the Battle of the Somme. The house was behind some bushes—it's a bungalow, actually; you can only see the telly aerial over the top of the hedge—and there was a sort of shed. Everything else was mud and trenches. The sky was grey and it was drizzling. There was thick orange water in the trenches and this big dip in the middle, like a shell crater. Any minute you expected someone to open up with a mortar or some guy in a tin hat leap over an embankment and whop you with an entrenching tool. I mean, remember when we went to the Imperial War Museum and they had those mock-ups of trench warfare?'

'Yeah,' Nina said, 'those spiked gloves and things. It looked more like the Middle Ages than seventy years ago.'

'Those mock-ups were dead cosy compared to Tokesby Holmes. You know, we were standing there, and the Land Rover was up to its axles, and I suddenly realized what it must have been like. I mean, you could feel yourself *rotting*. There wasn't any grass, nothing green at all, just mud and tree stumps. Every now and again something went plop, like gas coming out of a

48

swamp. I never saw anything like it. Usually when Dave does a landscape it's turf and rhododendrons and *Cupressus Leylandii*.'

'What's *Cupressus Leylandii*?' Nina asked.

'BL Tree Division,' Nazzer said.

'I said, "What have you been up to, Dave?" and he says, "It's not us, do us a favour, it's those silly sods up at the farm." Well, you know what it's like round here, they've got a thing about trees. I think it's a primitive race memory left over from the time when we were all plants.'

'Speak for yourself,' Nina said. 'Personally, I've never been a plant.'

'I meant the Common Ancestor.'

'I thought the Common Ancestor was some kind of orang-utan,' Nazzer said.

'It could just as easily have been a tree. I think it's deep-seated envy. As soon as any tree gets over six feet tall they cut it down. They don't even like hedges, much. If a hedge looks like it's doing too well for itself, they grub it up and put in ranch fencing or breeze-blocks; something that won't grow. Dave said, "They didn't leave it to us to clear the land, they did it themselves. Bloody townies." Then I realized it wasn't a farm at all, just a house on some land that *had* been a farm. Typical. The last trees in the area and they go and cut them down. Only they hadn't just chopped them down, they'd started digging the roots out and then found they couldn't manage it so they'd got Dave and Joe in to finish the job. The trees that were down were little ones—I think it had been a coppice. The one we had to deal with was an oak; well, it had been

49

an oak. There was only the roots left and about four feet of trunk—and a pile of ash. So we sort of swam over to have a look.

'"We'll need a tractor and chains for this," Dave says and then another voice says, "I said they shouldn't do it."

'I never jumped so high in my life. One moment there was just us and the mud, and then out of nowhere, this voice. So we looked up and there was this little kid, about ten, standing on the bank in the rain, wearing an oilskin and sou'wester and boots. You could tell he wasn't local, the local kids wear camouflage gear and balaclava helmets, like the IRA. This one looked more like Christopher Robin.'

'Your sister's boy?'

'No, Christopher Robin from *Winnie the Pooh*. You know, with Eeyore and Piglet.'

'Funny friends, you've got,' Nazzer said.

'It's a *book*,' Nina said. 'They all lived in a tree and pretended to be clouds.'

'Funny reading habits you've got.'

'Well, he just stood there, looking at us, and Dave said, "Come again?" and this little kid says, "I told them not to do it."

'"What's your name, then?" Dave says, and the little kid says, "Sebastian," and Dave says, "Well, you come down here, Sebastian. You make me nervous up there. That bank's going to give way at any moment." So Sebastian came down. He jumped. There was this puddle in the crater right next to us and he jumped into it. Dave said, "I asked for that," so I just wiped the mud off my tonsils and didn't kill anyone.

'Sebastian says, "That was my camp."

'"Played soldiers, did you?" Dave says. "With your mates?"

'"I haven't got any mates," Sebastian says. He didn't sound sad, he was just telling us. "My mates are at St Radigund's. I don't know anybody here."

'"Where's St Radigund's?" Dave says.

'"Near Canterbury," says Sebastian. Then I realized he must go away to school. I felt really sorry for him, I can tell you. All his friends at the other end of the country and him stuck there for weeks on end in No Man's Land.

'"Are you on half-term, then?" I said, and he nodded. *Then* he started looking sad. "I came back on Friday night," he said. "It was all dark, so I didn't come out here till this morning. Mummy said what they'd done but I didn't know what it would look like."

'Dave looked interested. He said, "Do you know what happened to Joe?"

'Sebastian said, "Who's Joe?"

'Dave said, "He's my partner. He was here yesterday."

'Sebastian gave us a very funny look. He said, "Did you do all this? You and Joe?"

'I think Dave caught on then, that while Sebastian was away at St Radigund's, getting educated, his loving parents had moved in with a chain saw and flattened his camp. "No," he says, very quickly, "we didn't do any of it. Mr Phillips—he your dad?"

'"Yes," says Sebastian, the way you might say, "Yes, I've got diphtheria."

'"Your dad started clearing this hollow to make an alpine garden," says Dave, though it looked more like an alpine bog to me, "only he's having a bit of trouble shifting the tree roots, so he called us in. We're landscape gardeners."

'"What's a landscape gardener?" says the lad.

'"Well, we do gardens on a big scale," says Dave. "We're used to moving earth and tree roots; we've got the equipment. We'd probably have made a better job of it than your old dad." He couldn't resist saying that, I could see.

'Sebastian says, "What happened to Joe?" and he had that funny look again, like he had a very good idea what had happened to Joe.

'Dave said, "He had a bit of an accident. He came over here yesterday afternoon to see what needed doing. Your dad was going to show him round the potholes, like."

'"What sort of an accident?" says Sebastian.

'"Well, we don't rightly know," says Dave. "He looks like he's been stung quite badly. We wondered whether your dad had been using pesticides."

'"What's pesticides?" says Sebastian. *Definitely* not local. I don't know what they teach them at St Radigund's.

'"Poisons," I said. "Poisons for insects."

'"Oh, yes," says the lad. "Daddy used some poison last week. And he got stung, too. Yesterday. When Mummy and me came back last night he was in bed, all swollen up."

'And he laughed. I didn't think it was very nice, laughing because your dad's all swollen up, but then I

52

remembered what Sebastian's dad had done to his camp.

'Dave was getting a bit worried by now. He says, "Does your dad know what stung him?" and Sebastian says, "No, but I do," and then he says again, "I told him he shouldn't do it."

'Dave got very serious. He squats down in the mud in front of the lad and he says, "Look, son, this could be dangerous. What do you know?"

'Sebastian didn't say anything for a bit. He just stood there, we all stood there, in the rain. It was coming on harder, running down our faces, only Sebastian was under his sou'wester. It wasn't rain running down *his* face. Then he said, "It was *my* camp. It was *my* tree. It was *my* bees."

'Dave says, "Bees? At this time of year?"

'Sebastian says, "They go to sleep in winter. He didn't dare do it in the summer. They were *savage* bees."

'Dave looked at me. He looked at Sebastian. He says, "There's no sense in us getting soaked, come and sit in the cab."

'We went back to the Land Rover, with Sebastian sitting between us. He took his sou'wester off and we got a good look at him. He didn't look the sort who'd go to prep school. He looked more the type that gets taken into Care.

'He said, "We get a train back to London for holidays. Mummy met me at Charing Cross. She said I mustn't be upset but Daddy had cleared the trees out of the hollow ready for planting the alpine garden. And I said he shouldn't have done that. I told him not to do it at Christmas but he said there were plenty of other places to play in the country, but there aren't. It's all sugar beet. I liked it when we lived in Cambridge; there were parks. I told Daddy not to cut down the oak tree because it was sacred."

'I thought, 'ere 'ere, pagan rites, but Sebastian says, "I thought he might leave it alone if I said it was sacred, but he said it was rotten. He said we'd plant a Japanese maple there if I minded so much, but the oak must go. So I had to tell the bees."

'"Are these imaginary bees, son?" Dave says, and Sebastian says, "No. They were wild bees and they lived in a hole in the oak tree. I told them what Daddy was going to do."

'"Ho, yes," says Dave, the way you do when little kids talk about fairies at the bottom of the dustbin.

'"Don't you know about bees?" says Sebastian. "If you keep bees, you have to tell them things."'

'Bedtime stories?' Nina said.

'No,' Nazzer said. 'Our neighbours when we lived at Hoveton had a couple of hives. If anything important happened Mrs Hooper used to trot down the garden to tell the bees. We'd see her sometimes yakking away nineteen to the dozen, first thing in the morning, before the bees got up. She said they'd sulk otherwise. It wasn't election results, or international crises, just things like auntie popping off or the time they won on the Premium Bonds.'

'Oh, folklore,' Nina said.

'Maybe, but he was a systems analyst and she wrote physics text books. You couldn't call them superstitious,' Nazzer said, 'but they had a lot of time for those bees.'

Maurice said, 'That's what Sebastian thought. He said he always told the bees if anything was going on and when he found that his dad was going to cut down their tree he went out and warned them. "They weren't hibernating," he said, "they were too savage for that, they were just asleep. It was a bit after Christmas and icy cold, but I went and woke them up. If you looked down the hole into the rotten bit you could see the old brown wax combs poking out. I broke a bit off as a signal and then I could hear them *growling*, right down inside the tree. But as soon as I spoke they knew it was me so they didn't come out." They were very fierce, he said, but they never stung *him*. Apparently they used to hang around the tree in summer and zap anyone who came near, just for kicks, not self defence, but never Sebastian. He said he told them they were in danger. He hoped they'd take the hint and fly away but of course, it was the wrong time of year for them to swarm, so they were still there when Daddy came along with his saw.

'His mum broke it to him while they were driving back from London. As soon as Daddy began sawing the bees woke up and started making threatening noises, what Sebastian called growling, so he went back to the house and got some kind of poison and poured it into the hollow. I don't know what it was but it finished off the bees. Next day he went out again, cut down the tree and burned the trunk.

'"Is that them there ashes?" Dave says. Sebastian says yes, and started crying again. We didn't know what to do, really. He wasn't the sort of little lad you could pat on the head and say there there to.

'"He burned the nest?" says Dave.

'"He burned the *bees*," says Sebastian. "They were in the tree and he burned them. Last year he poured boiling water on the *ants*. He poisoned the *moles*." I can tell you,' Maurice said, 'I was getting very glad this guy had swelled up. I said to Sebastian, "Look, if he put poison in the holes, the bees would have been dead before he burned them. They wouldn't have known about it."

'"They knew who did it, though," Sebastian said. "I warned them. That's why they stung him."

'"When did they sting him?"

'"Yesterday," he says, "while Mummy was fetching me from London. He came out here with your friend Joe and they were waiting for him. I'm sorry they got Joe, but they never did like strangers." He climbed over my knees and got out of the Land Rover. It had stopped raining and he stood there in a puddle, looking in. "And they'll get you," he says. "You'd better keep away." And he ran off up the bank towards the bungalow. Dave looks at me and screws a finger into his forehead.

'"D'you reckon St Radigund's is a special school?" he says. I sort of shrugged. I mean,' Maurice said, 'I didn't think Sebastian was a nutter, but he gave me the creeps. "Oh well," says Dave, "let's get out and have a recce while the rain holds off," so we climbed out again and sloshed over to the oak stump. Sebastian had disappeared, it was all quiet except for water dripping off the shed. It was a little black tarred shack with a thatched roof.

'"We'll dig in underneath and loosen it a bit," Dave says. "Better take an axe to those roots." He stood back, the way you do before going into action, right into the middle of the pile of ash, and that was when we heard it.'

'Heard what?'

'Just like Sebastian said, a sort of growling, only it wasn't really growling but it was threatening, all right. And you couldn't tell where it was coming from, but it was close. Dave says, "What in heck is that?" and then he yelled and slapped the back of his neck and started flapping his arms. I knew what it was on account of Sebastian, but you could see how they'd taken Joe and old man Phillips by surprise. Then they started on me; I could feel them up my sleeves and down my neck; *crawling*. We both turned round and belted back to the Land Rover and the buzzing came with us. Dave got it worse than me because he'd been standing right in the middle of the ashes. What you might call the heart of the problem,' Maurice said. 'Live bees can only sting once, but after they're dead I suppose they can go on as long as they like. We sat in the Land Rover yelling and slapping like a pair of loonies and then Dave started it up and began to back out towards the road. You could hear the buzzing above the engine. It wasn't a sort of drowsy summer-day buzzing, either,' Maurice said. 'It was like Stukas. I looked out of the side window and there was Sebastian, back again, standing on the oak roots. Nothing was stinging *him*.

'"I'll tell old Phillips where he can put his tree stumps," says Dave, and the Land Rover's churning up mud behind like a muck spreader, and then just as we got clear, the shed collapsed. I thought for a moment we'd done it, I mean, that was impossible, but that's what it looked like. It came down slowly; first the thatch slid off all in a lump, and then the walls fell outwards, like someone had given the thing a shove from underneath. Of course, I guessed by then it was nothing to do with us at all, and I thought the rain must have washed away the foundations,' Maurice said, 'but once the walls were down you could see this mound in the middle where the floor should have been. It could have been a pile of compost, I suppose, but it looked more to me like a socking great mole hill.

'Dave saw it too. He revs up and yells, "Let's get out of here before he calls in the ants!" I don't reckon Sebastian was telling the truth when he said that all his mates were at St Radigund's,' Maurice said. 'Not *all* of them.'

'It depends on what you mean by mates,' Nazzer said.

4

DRUG-CRAZED THUGS WRECKED MY LOUNGE — Exclusive

'I don't care how much you fancy her,' Nina said. 'I'm not giving you her address.'

'There are ways of finding out,' Maurice said. 'Ve haff ways of making you talk.'

'We even have ways of making you shut up,' Nazzer sighed. 'None of them noticeably successful.'

'You don't want to get involved with Claire, she's Bad News,' Nina said. 'She's trouble.'

'Funny, isn't it,' Maurice said. 'Have you noticed that when you particularly want to do something, some creep always comes along and says, "You don't want to do that"?'

'What sort of trouble?' Nazzer said. 'If you're trying to put him off, Nina, I don't think you're going the right way about it. If you'd said, "My cousin Claire is beautiful, accomplished, witty, extremely sexy and moreover her legs go all the way to the top," he'd have got very suspicious and demanded to know what was *really* wrong with her.'

'She isn't sexy,' Nina said. 'That's the trouble.'

'I think you might let me find out for myself,' Maurice said. 'I am not particularly inexperienced in these matters.'

'You don't need experience with Claire. You need an interesting book to help pass the time. Look, I *know*,' Nina said. 'I've seen her at home. I went to stay with her just before Easter.'

'Where?'

'Never mind where, you won't be going — no you *won't*, Maurice. Her old man'd never let you over the doorstep for a start.'

'This old man being your uncle? Aha! You've only got one uncle. A simple process of deduction, Watson—'

'Not *that* uncle. He isn't really my uncle anyway. Claire's only a second cousin—I don't know what you'd call him; a sort of uncle twice removed. If he was ten times removed it couldn't be far enough,' Nina said. 'They're a bit old for parents, I mean, they had her late and she's the only one, and they've got this thing about protecting her from corrupting influences.'

'How come they let her knock around with you, then?'

'They don't,' Nina said. 'They reckon that what happened at Easter was all my fault. Well, it was in a way because if I hadn't been there it wouldn't have happened, but it only happened because they let it, it's just that they wouldn't have let it happen if I *hadn't* been there. I mean,' Nina said, 'believe it or not, they don't like going out and leaving her alone in the evening. But they thought the two of us would be safe and sort of extorted promises with menace about not answering the door or the phone.'

'Why not the phone?'

'I dunno. In case there was a man breathing on the other end, I suppose. They've read too many headlines—you know: I WAS A TEENAGE SCHOOLGIRL —EXCLUSIVE.'

'You get these throw-backs,' Nazzer said. 'Think about it; these people must have lived through the Swinging Sixties. If we are to believe what we hear about the Swinging Sixties, it was ten years of purple haze with yellow spots. It was rock, surf and Acid. It was Liverpool—'

'Mini skirts.'

'Don't you ever think of anything but legs?'

'Tambourines, Chelsea boots, love—'

'Money.'

'Odd about the money. I wonder where it went?'

'My point is,' Nazzer said, 'by all accounts the Sixties were something of which you could not remain unaware. They went on for a long time—'

'Almost as long as the Seventies.'

'And yet you get these pockets of resistance, people who came through it all absolutely untouched, went into a kind of space warp and leapt from 1959 straight to 1970. I've got this snapshot of my father wearing enormous trousers—'

'He still wears enormous trousers.'

'These were enormous round the turn-ups. And Mum with white lips, looking like a corpse that's had second thoughts, and they still go into embarrassing postures when certain records get played on the radio. It obviously had a lasting effect on them, like the First World War, but there are people, Claire's parents for instance, who behave as though it never happened.'

'I don't think it ever did,' Maurice said. 'I think it was collective hysteria, a sort of mass hallucination, like the Indian Rope Trick. If you credit half of what you see on telly, everyone was hallucinating anyway —including the Government,' he added.

'A lot of people say the Sixties didn't end till 1970 anyway, like the Seventies ended with 1980. There's all these rows about whether the next century starts in the year 2000 or not.'

'This century ends in the year 2000,' Maurice said. 'The next one starts in 2001. The First Century started with the year One, didn't it? BC ended with God pressing a button and sending the trip meter back to a row of noughts.'

'Well, all right,' Nina said, 'but Claire's parents were definitely in cold storage during the Sixties. They were probably having a private Forties revival at the time.'

'Getting in training for the Eighties backlash,' Maurice said.

'Well, as soon as Claire's mum and dad had got clear, she sent me down to the corner shop to buy nibbles. She wanted me to try the off-licence, but I wouldn't.'

'For nibbles?'

'For booze.'

'Oh, how noble,' Nazzer said. ' "I cannot tell a lie," you said to the salesman. "I am under eighteen".'

'It wasn't that. No one ever asks if I'm eighteen,' Nina said, 'not since I was fourteen. But Claire had asked these guys in from school and I didn't want trouble—not with *her* parents. Claire gets stoned on shandy.'

'Look, I *must* meet her,' Maurice said, urgently. 'This could be a financial breakthrough.'

'That's not what I meant. She could get stoned on cornflakes if she put her mind to it. Soon as I came back with the nibbles I could see something was going on. They've got these cream curtains in the front room, that let the light through, and right down the street I could see the light had turned a sort of dull red. She'd turned off the lamp in the middle and got down all the bedside lights, set out round the edge of the room with red cloth over the shades, what she probably thought was sinful, only the red cloth was a sports shirt and a mini slip and a pink shower cap with a frill. "That'll melt," I said. "We'll have it turned off by the time it gets to melting point," Claire said, and sniggered. Enough to make you puke,' Nina said. 'She'd got all the coffee tables out of their nest and set out those little paté bowls you get from the Co-op—for the nibbles. I'd got olives and cashew nuts, but she had out these wizened sausages on sticks. It all looked a bit dangerous to me.'

'The sausages?'

'No, they just looked nasty. But you couldn't move for bedside lamps, and coffee tables catching you behind the knees. They've got a horrible big glass coffee table too, with bamboo legs, that was up against the wall with a chess set and a row of bottles on it. I said, "Hadn't you better put those away," and she said, "Hell, no, I've only just got them out," sounding really phony. And the drink looked phony too. It wasn't whisky and gin and vodka—well, there was whisky, but the rest was all horrible colours. One of them looked like copper sulphate.'

'Curaçao,' Maurice said. 'It tastes of orange. It's a bit of a shock when you swallow it. I mean, you're *expecting* copper sulphate.'

'And something really foul-looking in a green bottle shaped like a mermaid. I couldn't see which end of the mermaid the drink came out. I started wondering about these fellows she'd invited; Chris and Stu—I'd met them before. I mean, I could imagine what would happen if one of *you* got your hands on that mermaid.'

'It would be creative though,' Nazzer said. 'We wouldn't do anything vulgar, would we, Maurice?'

'We'd got the central heating going full blast, and then Claire put the fire on. It was an electric coal fire, with imitation flickers.'

'I hate those,' Maurice said. 'If you watch long enough you can see the same flicker coming round, over and over again. It must be like a lighthouse inside, only faster.'

'And Claire had draped things all over the settees—scarves and shawls and that, and found about fifteen cushions to sling around. One of them was a pink plush thing and I said, "You'd better put this away," and she said "Why?" and I said, "Because it looks like a fat stomach with a belly button." I didn't fancy Chris or Stu thinking the same thing, half-way through the evening. But Claire just gave this snigger and put the belly cushion right on top of the pile where no one could miss it. I suppose she'd decided to live dangerously.'

'She gets her kicks from cushions?'

'If you had parents like hers, even two thick oafs like Chris and Stu would look dangerous. Well, it was getting on for nine by now, and I thought that if these two didn't turn up soon it would hardly be worth their while turning up at all, because Claire's parents' idea of an evening out is an *evening* out. Evening ends at ten, on their clock. Then it's night. Actually,' Nina said, 'I was hoping they wouldn't come. I could see what Claire had in mind. She had this tiny dress on—I don't know where she'd managed to get anything that small, it may have been a sweater, and she kept stretching, and every time she stretched it got smaller.'

'Look, what's all this *purity* all of a sudden?' Maurice demanded. 'What's all this disapproving of blokes and booze and carnal knowledge?'

'*I* don't mind carnal knowledge,' Nina said. 'I like carnal knowledge. But this was carnal ignorance. Claire looked out through the curtains—that was another stretch and the dress almost disappeared—and there were these two figures in parkas, out in the street, dancing very slowly round a lamp post, knees up, knees up, sort of like Eskimo cannibals. "What the *hell* are they doing?" says Claire. "Keeping warm?" I said and she said, "Like hell." I could tell,' said Nina, 'that she'd got this idea that Hell is a very bad word. So I said, "Perhaps they're trying to work up courage."

'"*Them* two?" she says—she wouldn't say that normally. She's been brought up to talk *nacely*—

65

"Them two?" she says; "go and tell them to come in," so I said, "You go," and she said, "I'll freeze in this," and sort of shrugged her weeny garment till it got even weenier. "You've got leggings on," she said. "I should take them off later," she said, and made that really nasty noise again, like a smirk, only you could hear it.'

'By the time I got to the door so had they, Chris and Stu. They were leaning on it, and when I turned the catch they fell in on me, Stu did, anyway. Chris fell straight past and hit his head on the banisters. "Well, don't just stand there, come in," says Claire. She was *posing* in the doorway of the lounge and I suppose she had that line already rehearsed. I mean, they *were* in. Chris was so far in he was almost out the back door, but she didn't seem to have noticed. I left them to it and went into the lounge and got a shawl and threw it over the row of bottles. I didn't want to be around afterwards when Claire's dad found out how much was left in them. There was a lot of creaking out in the hall as they took off their parkas—'

'*Parkas?*' Nazzer said. 'This is all getting to sound distinctly *quaint*. What were they wearing underneath? Bondage gear?'

'There's nowhere to go but backwards,' Maurice said. 'Bondage gear looked like the end, didn't it?'

'It was,' Nazzer said. 'Nothing's topped it. Personality's down to skin level, now, sort of designer filth.'

'So they all came in and Claire says, "Let's have a drink." She looked very ratty at me and pulled the shawl off the bottles again. Stu said he'd have coffee because he'd got cold hanging about outside and Claire said, "Well, you didn't have to spend half the evening dancing round the lamp post. Have a whisky. It's more warming."

'Stu said, "We got here too early. We thought you might not be ready," and Chris says, "Like not dressed," and laughed, like Claire's smirk, only worse.'

'A kind of audible leer?' Nazzer suggested.

'That's it. So Claire asked *me* to go and make coffee and just as I was going out she said, "What'll you have, Chris?" and I thought, Here we go, because Chris would probably want something inflammatory like a Vodka Cinzano with Ribena, or worse. But he said, "I'll have coffee too. All me extremities are turning blue and shrunken." I knew what he meant, but she didn't. She misses a lot, really. I said, "What'll you have, Claire?" and she said, "I suppose I'd better have coffee, too." She was really scowling, now, and I nipped out quick before she asked me to make it Irish coffee. Come to think of it,' Nina said, 'I could have given them hot paraffin and Bisto and *told* them it was Irish coffee and they wouldn't have known any different.'

'When I came back with the coffee they were all sitting there looking stuffed. Chris and Stu on one settee and Claire on the other, sort of flirting with the scarf. There wasn't anything else to flirt with.'

'Hang on,' Nazzer said. '*Two* settees? Imitation coal fire? A mermaid? What kind of *ambiance* are these people aiming for?'

'They call them sofas,' Nina explained, 'Claire's

parents do. But you can't disguise a settee. It's got settee written all over it.'

'It's that fat middle-aged look they have,' Maurice said. 'Even when they're new.'

'Claire put a record on, disco music, very ancient, only the music centre was behind the settee so all you could hear was a kind of thump thump thump, dead quiet so the neighbours wouldn't hear and come round to grass later, and this thin yelling noise in the background like some tiny mad person was trapped inside the settee and trying to get out. I think it was the only record Claire's got. She must have smuggled it in disguised as a plate. Her mum and dad have got lots but they all seem to be old men singing *I Did it My Way* on one note.'

'Strange how people get this compulsion to sing *I Did it My Way* when they reach a certain age,' Maurice remarked. 'Like they were afraid you might think they hadn't done anything at all.'

'Or else that their way was just like everyone else's so nobody ever noticed them doing it,' Nazzer said. 'It only seems to be men, though. Women don't sing *I Did it My Way*.'

'Claire said, "Have an olive," and Chris said, "With coffee? Have a heart, Hawes." She hates being called Hawes. She doesn't like the sound of it. "It would be all right with Vermouth," she says, all sophisticated.'

'I thought it was pronounced Ver*mooth*,' Nazzer said. 'Vermouth sounds like a seaside resort.'

'Vermouth rock,' Maurice said.

'"Have a peanut," says Claire. It got very quiet. You could hear peanuts being chewed. I tell you,'

Nina said, 'I began to wish that Mr and Mrs Hawes *would* come back, before we all turned to stone. "Have a drink," says Claire, when the peanuts had gone. "What you got?" says Chris, getting up to look, and he fell over the coffee table, the one where Claire's dad keeps his chess set.

'"Have a whisky," says Claire. At least she'd had the sense not to start drinking before they did. "Look at this, Stu," says Chris. "It's not an ordinary chess set. It's all little people."

'"It's the Isle of Lewis chess set," says Stu. "You know, the one they dug up in the Hebrides that was hundreds of years old."

'"So what's your dad doing with it?" says Chris. "Is it hot? Did he nick it from the British Museum? I never knew your dad was a fence, Hawes."'

'I begin to feel that this Chris is not really our sort of person,' Nazzer said. 'His wit kind of gets you over the back of the neck with a dull thud.'

'Claire was getting really panicky because Chris was shunting the chess men about and her dad's dead fussy about his collectors' items. He orders them from the Sunday supplements and they're all made of resin, but he keeps them locked up in a cabinet. Only he does play chess, it's about the fastest thing he can manage, I think,' Nina said, 'so that's why the set had been left out. Chris was beginning to look mad. He says, "You want a game, Stu?" "Put them down," says Claire. She was geting furious now but Chris says, "I can't. I'm hooked. Aaaaah!" he says, "you should never have let me see them." He was down on his knees and sort of wrestling with a bishop. "I thought I was cured," he says, "but they're right. You're never cured of chess. I gotta play. I gotta play."

'Stu says, "Lay off, Stilwell," but he wouldn't. He was writhing about on the floor with a knight between his teeth. Claire began kicking him but he just kept moaning, "Cold Turkey! I gotta play. Gimme a fix."

'I said, "Haven't you got any ordinary chess men?" and I started collecting up the other pieces before Chris got hold of them. Stu helped. He prised the bishop out of Chris's hand and gave it to me. It was like nicking a dummy off a baby. Chris screams, "You can't do this to me!" and starts clawing at Stu's leg. If he'd clawed *my* leg,' Nina said, 'I'd have booted him in the head, but Stu just said, "Oh, shut up, I'll find you something else to play with. I saw this film once where they played chess with miniatures." "Miniature whats?" says Chris and the knight fell out of his mouth so I grabbed it, quick. "Miniature drink bottles," Stu said, and I saw where he was looking. Mr Hawes keeps this collection of miniatures on the pelmet over the window. "Let's play with those," he says. "Every time you win a piece you have to drink it."

'I said, "They're all empty." I'd have thought Stu would have had more sense.

'"No they're not," says Claire. That's just what I would have expected from her. She climbed on to the settee and started scooping them down—and they *weren't* empty; you could tell by the clunking. She laid them out on the chess board and there weren't nearly enough. "Hang about," says Stu. He took the stuffed olives out of the paté bowl and wiped them, and put *them* out for pawns.

'"What about my prawns?" says Chris. "Pawns," says Stu. "Prunes," says Chris. "That's a thought," says Stu, "you got any prunes?" I thought things were getting a bit out of hand, myself,' Nina said, 'but Claire went stumping off to the kitchen. She'd have brought him pickled onions if he'd asked, she was so relieved *something* was happening. Chris started fossicking in the sideboard and got out the salt and pepper mill and said they'd be *his* king and queen.'

'What about the miniatures?' Maurice said.

'Well,' Nina said, 'that was it. They'd forgotten about them, so when Claire came back with the prunes *I* went out to the kitchen and grabbed everything I could find for rooks and bishops and knights—egg cups, spice jars, almond essence and a salad oil bottle. By the time we'd got that lot out there wasn't space for anything else. We'd got every piece, except for Stu's queen. He was looking round the room for a queen and he suddenly spotted the mermaid. There wasn't really room for her on the square but he squeezed all the other pieces sideways and plonked her down next to the salad oil bottle—that was his king. And the board was ready then. It looked like a fairy banquet—horrible bent fairies who'd been up all night boozing and gambling and smashing windows.'

'If you think about it,' Nazzer said, 'that's very much what fairies must have been like anyway. People seemed to spend most of their time buying them off, like they were running some kind of protection racket. You know the score, a note through the window, wrapped round a brick. *You have been a bit tight with the bread and milk lately, squire. Put one medium sliced and a*

71

pint of gold top behind the cistern or the lads will be round to do you over. Signed, Puck.'

'Stu says, "Your move," and Chris moved one of his prunes. Stu moved an olive. Chris moved another prune and Stu moved an olive and then Chris started going Vroom-vroom and zoomed his almond essence out of the back row and took it. And Stu said, "You can't do that with a knight," and Chris says, "It's not a knight, it's a bishop," and eats the olive, quick; and Stu says, "Bishops don't go there," and Chris says, "They do in *my* army." "Right, no holds barred," says Stu, and he got the mermaid by the throat and brought her down on one of the prunes. "Two can play at that game," he says.

'"Now eat it," says Chris. "Not likely," says Stu, and put the prune to one side, but Chris says, "I ate the olive. It was your idea." "I said we got to drink what we won," says Stu, but Chris said it was the same thing, so Stu ate the prune. Well, he just swallowed it. I don't think he knew that prunes have stones in,' Nina said. 'Anyway, Chris moved his pepper mill and took another olive and then Stu plunged in with the mermaid and captured the almond essence.

'"Now drink that," says Chris. "Get out of it," says Stu, but Chris said, "You won it, you drink it."'

'Stu exhibits a certain lack of foresight, on this showing, don't you think?' Nazzer observed. 'Which amounts almost to imbecility.'

'He kept saying that almond essence was poisonous,' Nina said. 'Actually, he didn't know it *was* almond essence, because it had *Ratafia* on the bottle. I don't think he can ever go into a kitchen. And Claire

72

says, "Go on, Chris, make him drink it," and drapes an arm round his neck like those women in old films who try and get the men to fight and won't have them back until they've been beaten to pulp, but Chris wasn't having any. "That's all I need," he said. "Chess groupies." "Count me out," I said. Chris yells, "Do you think Kasparov became World Champion with a woman hanging round his neck?"

'Stu took the lid off the almond essence and swigged. His eyes closed. I didn't even try to guess what it must taste like,' Nina said. 'Cyanide's the nearest, I suppose. Then Chris got his egg cup and took another olive and Stu says, "I've got you sussed, Stilwell. I see why you let me have all the goodies. Every time you take a piece you get a treat. Every time I do I get poisoned." "I'm after your mermaid," says Chris.

'Stu didn't say anything. He went over to the settee and got an armful of cushions, and set them up like sandbags at his end of the table. Then he moved the mermaid behind the sandbags. Chris's eyes got very small. He snaps his fingers at Claire. "Bring me a fork," he says.'

'I must say,' Maurice remarked, 'she does seem to bring out the worst in men. You haven't choked me off yet, you know.'

'You don't have to *bring* out the worst in Chris,' Nina said. 'It oozes out through his pores. I thought Chris wanted the fork to go after the mermaid with, but he laid the tines on the table, put a prune on the handle and twanged it. And the prune shot up in the air, over the sandbags.

'"Right," says Stu, "say your prayers, Stilwell,"

73

and he went over to the fireplace and fetched the poker.'

'I thought it was an electric fire,' Maurice said.

'It is,' Nina said, 'but they've got a poker and a shovel and a hearth brush all hung up from a stand, and this fancy coal bucket made of brass with a galleon on the side. Stu stood with his feet apart at his end of the table and swung the poker a few times and teed-off with an olive.'

' "Put that down!" says Claire. She was crawling about on the floor, looking for prunes, because Chris was firing at will. And Stu started yelling, "Now Stu Ballesteros will go for a hole in one!" and took another swing and hit the pepper mill. Chris goes, "Now eat that," but of course Stu wouldn't—'

'Why of course?' Nazzer inquired.

'—So Chris got the pepper mill and started grinding it over Stu's head.'

'You mentioned cannibals, earlier,' Nazzer said. 'Can we look forward to seeing Stu *eaten* in the next reel?'

'Stu rolled across the floor and stuck his head in the coal bucket—for safe keeping. When he stood up again he was wearing it. It came right down over his neck. Chris hit him over the head with the hearth brush and he sort of clanged and Stu was laying about with the poker and not hitting Chris because he couldn't see where he was going. Then he started doing robotic movements, all stiff and slow. "I am an android," he says. "I am Zenner Diode, curse of the great black hole in Orion. I am programmed to destroy the galaxy—starting with Stilwell."'

'That's quite good, really,' Maurice conceded. 'I like that—Zenner Diode. Is he into electronics?'

'What's electronics got to do with it?' Nina said. 'He fell over one of the coffee tables and Chris jumped on him. "I am Luke Skyscraper," he says. "I am going to zap you, Zenner Diode." Claire was still crawling about looking for prunes. She was really in a snot, now. "I thought you were supposed to be playing *chess*," she says, and Stu goes, "This is Galactic Chess," and Chris goes, "Kamikaze Chess!" and spread his arms and dived on Stu and they both hit the floor with this terrible clang from the coal bucket. Claire lost her rag and grabbed the poker and started whanging the coal bucket and screaming "Get up! Get out!" We didn't hear the door open.

'None of us noticed anything,' Nina said, 'until this voice comes out of the coal bucket: "I can see four little feet, all in a row," and we looked round and saw the feet, and the legs, and Mr and Mrs Hawes standing in the doorway. Claire stood up. Her eyes went all swivelly and frightened. I was glad she had the poker and not me because the coal bucket was all over dents. Chris came out from behind the cushions and Stu climbed out of the coal bucket. Mrs Hawes said, "You're drunk."

'Claire started to say no, but her dad sort of turned on her and she shut up. "You've been drinking," says Mrs Hawes, and this time Chris said no but he started hiccuping—from shock probably. That didn't help. It came out no-ho-ho-ho-ho.

'"You have," says Claire's dad and she said, "We haven't. Look at the bottles. They haven't been

75

opened. Even the open ones aren't open."

'"You've had something," says her mum, and Stu says, "Ratafia," and you could smell it. You could smell something else, too, but we didn't know what it was. Mr and Mrs Hawes noticed, because they started sniffing. I know what *they* thought it was, though. They'd heard about young tearaways and drink-and-drugs parties, you could tell. Old man Hawes is a PE teacher. *He* knows how to deal with young tearaways. "You've been taking—*things*," he says, like he knew all about it so there was no point in us arguing. "Substances," he says. "Where do you get them? Who supplies you?" Stu woke up then, when Mr Hawes said supplies. He suddenly realized what Hawes was on about. "You mean you think we're stoned?" he says. "I mean," says Hawes, "if you haven't been drinking you must have been taking something. What was it?" Chris just goes "U-hurk!" but Stu was furious. He said, "We haven't been taking anything." "Don't lie to me, boy," says Hawes, and you could just imagine him in the gym, being God in a track suit. "How else did you get into this state?" And we all looked round, then. You could see what he meant. There were cushions all over the place and scarves, and the carpet was covered with prunes and olives and egg cups, and the mermaid was leaking all over the rug, and there was this *smell*, almonds and something else, that Claire's mum and dad thought was pot or heroin. Stu sort of mumbled, "I dunno. Must have been adrenalin or something." Nobody said anything. I mean, the room looked like elephants had been *raped* in it. No way could you blame that on adrenalin. But

Claire thought her mum and dad didn't know what Stu was talking about, though there must be plenty of adrenalin in PE. She says, "It's an enzyme."

'They didn't believe her. Mrs Hawes started crying and Mr Hawes clouted Claire and Claire started crying. Chris and Stu were offering to clear up but I thought it would be better if they just went, so I saw them out. They seemed to sober up on the doorstep. I suppose it was the fresh air,' Nina said, 'only of course, they *were* sober. Mind you,' said Nina, 'I'd hate to meet them if they really were stoned.'

'It's a hormone,' Maurice said.

'What?'

'Adrenalin's a hormone. Produced by the adrenal gland, downwind of the kidneys.'

'My god,' Nina said, 'it's a good thing Claire got that wrong. If her mum and dad had known there were hormones involved they'd have called the Vice Squad in. That funny smell, though—it was the mermaid. I'm glad they never tried drinking her; she was full of aftershave.'

'I think innocence in adults is terrifying,' Nazzer said.

5

Like Immortality Almost

'It must have been about the time we had the Everlasting Hamster,' Nazzer said.

'The Everlasting what?'

'You must remember the strange case of the Everlasting Hamster. Every school has one.'

'Not ours.'

'First schools.'

'We had a perfectly ordinary hamster at our school,' Nina said. 'It was white. Thick as two short furry planks, but it was dead normal.'

'That's what you think,' Nazzer said. 'That's what you were meant to think. How long did you have it?'

'It was there all the time I was in the Infants,' Nina said. 'Actually, they still had it when I went to the Middle School, because I came back for a visit and it was still there. We called it Snowball,' said Nina.

'Hamsters live about two years, and that's pushing it,' Maurice said. 'It's the soft living rots their moral fibre.'

'The pressures are tremendous, though,' Nazzer said.

'The pressures of being a hamster?'

'The pressures of being a school hamster. When people complain that teachers only work five hours a week and have long holidays, they always say, Ah, but the pressures are tremendous.'

'Wild hamsters probably have long stringy hind legs and powerful muscles,' Maurice said. 'Like Cumbrian sheep. Those hill sheep are rugged individualists; they think for themselves. They don't hang around in bunches waiting for someone else to take the initiative.'

'Like you said, hamsters lead very short lives— from being naturally sheep-like, I suppose,' Nazzer said. 'How come school hamsters live forever?'

'It must be the long holidays,' Nina said.

'They've drunk at the spring of eternal youth,' Maurice suggested. 'All that exposure to extreme childhood.'

'It's a conspiracy,' Nazzer said. 'It's to protect us from coming to terms with death too early. There's this class of little kids, for instance, who think they were found under gooseberry bushes and that God came for Great Grandma on a fluffy white cloud, and in comes this young teacher—'

'More likely a student,' Nina said. 'Students are dead keen on bringing live specimens into the class-room. Then they take you round a farm.'

'Ours didn't,' Maurice said. 'Our student took us over East Ruston Tip—with a real dustman. God, we knew how to live in those days,' said Maurice.

'In comes this young student—'

'One of our students brought in baby chicks,' Nina said. 'The first time he brought them in they were a day old, all yellow and soft. The next day they were a bit bigger, but by the third day they were huge. They had great vulture claws and wing feathers. Then they started getting smaller again.'

'What did you end up with?' Maurice asked. 'Eggs?'

'No, don't you see, he—this student—was getting them from his lab at college to show us how they developed, only the lab assistants were giving him a different set of chickens each day.'

'Oh, well, the Everlasting Hamster trick has to be done more carefully,' Nazzer said. 'Like I was saying, you've got this young teacher—or student, Nina—brings in a nice hamster for the reception class. Well, the *next* reception class inherits it, and they all love it, and then one day it gets a bit sluggish; sort of indifferent to the sunflower seeds, and then it drops dead overnight. So what happens? Teacher rushes out and buys an identical one, or the kiddiwinks will weep. Next morning, there's little Hammy, back on the wheel kick and doing press-ups, feeling a new hamster, as you might say. "Oh look, children," says Miss. "Hammy's got better during the night." Couple of years later Hammy Mark Two cashes in his chips and the same thing happens again. Don't tell *me*,' Nazzer said, heavily. 'I have actually performed the Everlasting Hamster trick.'

'It's not worth it, though,' Nina said.

'What's not?'

'Trying to protect little kids from knowing about death. We had this big carp in the school pond and nobody took any notice of it until we came in one morning and it was floating on the top. It was Jason Hales that spotted it. "Oh look, Miss," he says. "Jaws is dead."'

'Jaws? Is that what you called it?' Maurice said.

'Odds-on half the goldfish in this country are called Jaws,' Nazzer said. 'Like pet pussy-cats are called Fang.'

'What was the hamster called?' Maurice asked. 'Rambo?'

'Cedric,' Nazzer said.

'Cedric the Hamster?'

'After Little Lord Fauntleroy. It had long golden hair. So had he.'

'What's Little Lord Fauntleroy got to do with it?'

'He was called Cedric too, apparently,' Nazzer explained. 'This teacher—'

'Which teacher?'

'The one my brother had in the Infants. She read a lot, this teacher. It was the long golden hair that caused all the trouble.'

'Anyway,' Nina said, 'when we found poor old Jaws floating about we went and fetched Miss Lovell and she comes out and says, "It's all right, children, he's just having a little sleep." So we said, "No, Miss, he's dead," but she wouldn't have it. "He's just sleeping," she says. Well, then someone noticed his head had been bitten off—it was probably the caretaker's cat, but we didn't want to upset old Miss Lovell, I mean, *that's* why little kids don't like death. It's embarrassing. So Lisa-Marie Hodges says, "I expect Jesus came for him, Miss."'

'You'd think Jesus would have something better to do than hang around school ponds biting the heads off fish,' Maurice remarked.

'That was what *we* thought, but Miss Lovell seemed

81

to believe that must be the right explanation, so we had a funeral. I mean, she had to admit that he wasn't just dossing down with his head off, and then we all had to go and write about it in our news books and draw a picture. You know, *Today Jaws went to join the angels*, and there's all these crayon pictures of Jaws with wings and a halo, even though he didn't have a head in most of them. Jason got wrong, though. He drew a head and then gave him horns and a pitchfork. Miss Lovell,' said Nina, 'thought that was not nice.'

'Did Cedric have his head bitten off as well?' Maurice said.

'Not so's you'd notice,' Nazzer said. 'Cedric had come to the end of his natural span, so to speak. He turned up—'

'Oh, I get it. There was this ring at the bell and there's Cedric on the doorstep with his little furry suitcase. "I've come home to die," he says.'

'He came home for half-term,' said Nazzer. 'You know how it is, everyone takes turns at entertaining the livestock for the weekend. Well, my brother got chosen to have Cedric over half-term. He was high on it for a week in advance, making little beds in shoeboxes and that. We kept telling him that Cedric would have to stay in his cage but he'd practically built a hamster Hilton by the time Friday came. I had to stop off at the First School on the way home and make sure they both got back all right. Mark didn't just have Cedric, there was his football and bomber jacket—'

'Cedric's?'

'Mark's. And this great roll of paper.'

'Oh, the art work,' Nina said. 'Do you remember

art in the Infants? Great stiff brushes with all the whiskers coming out, and that sticky paint; doesn't matter what colour it starts out, it always ends up purple.'

'There's probably a DES directive,' Maurice said. 'First School paint has to have a specific viscosity on account of little kids really being unable to express themselves unless they can paint pictures with a fork dipped in raspberry instant whip.'

'On blotting paper.'

'Stands to reason,' Nazzer said, 'since the felt-tip revolution people have stopped using ink. There must have been huge reserves of Government blotting paper left over when the dip pen went out of fashion, a sort of EEC pulp mountain. I reckon they sprayed it with something and sent it out to First Schools to paint on. Anyway, there's Mark with all his gear, waiting on the step, and this little cage under his arm with a heap of fluff and wood wool inside it.

'"Cedric's asleep," says Mark, well, he was whispering, so as not to wake Cedric up, although there were juggernauts thundering past ten metres away. I was going to carry the cage but Mark wouldn't leave go of it, so I had to carry the football and the pictures and the jacket. I had to carry all my own stuff, too, and push my bike. I was dead embarrassed—you know how it is when you're fourteen. I was afraid we'd run into one of my mates and they'd think I'd done the pictures. I didn't really like being seen with Mark anyway. I was very image-conscious in those days,' Nazzer admitted.

'Which of course you aren't now,' Maurice said.

'It was the Dagenham effect,' Nazzer said. 'You gotta be street-wise down in The Smoke. That is, you don't go walkies with your hamster, not if you wish to retain your credibility intact. Mark wasn't born till after we moved to Norfolk. He hadn't hardened off.

'Well, we got home and I put the cage on the table and Mark wants him out. Mum wasn't too keen on account of she was trying to lay out the tea things and hamsters can be pretty incontinent—'

'They what?'

'They do not put up their little furry paws and say "Please may I be excused?" But anyway, she said OK, just for a moment, so Mark opened the cage and gave us this long lecture on how to pick up a hamster, and out comes Cedric. I didn't feel too optimistic when I saw him,' Nazzer said. 'He looked as if he had things on his mind.'

'Hamsters don't have a lot of mind to have things on,' Nina said. 'Hamsters operate at a fairly primitive level.'

'Cedric didn't seem to be operating at all,' Nazzer said. 'After a few minutes he opened his eyes, but everything was in slow motion. He went for a bit of a stroll round the teapot, but it took him ages. He didn't look as if he was enjoying it and he went to sleep twice on the way back.

'"It's the fresh air," says Mum. "The journey home must have tired him out." Mark was getting worried. He'd brought back this bag of hamster nosh and he kept offering Cedric sunflower seeds and peanuts—and you could see Cedric was trying. He'd pick them up and fiddle with them like he wasn't quite sure how they worked but didn't want to let on. He even put a peanut in his pouch and took it round the teapot, and then he thought What the hell? and spat it out. I thought then, Hello, I thought; Cedric is not long for this world, but Mark kept stroking him and making those daft chicken noises like you do at little furry etceteras, and we knew we were in for a scene if Cedric popped his clogs over the holiday.

'"You put him to bye-byes," I said. "He'll have livened up by the morning."

'So we had tea, but Mark kept getting up and checking out the small and furry. He'd gone to earth again, under the wood wool and carpet fluff, but you could just see a bit of the long golden hair poking out.'

'Was he angora?' Nina said. 'You can get angora guinea-pigs. They look like sawn-off draught excluders, but I never saw an angora hamster.'

'Not *long* hair, exactly,' Nazzer said, 'but very lush. Only on account of his great age he did look a bit like the moths had been at him.

'Well, we got Mark off to bed, and he only came down about six times to make sure that Cedric was still, as you might say, on an earthly plane. He went to sleep in the end—'

'Cedric?'

'Mark. Cedric was already in a coma, as far as I could see. Mum says, "I think you might go along to that pet shop down Dereham Road tomorrow." "What for?" I said. "Medicine? He's past medicine," I said.

'"Quite," says Mum. "I think we may have to find a replacement."

'I went and looked under the wood wool. There didn't seem to be a lot going on. I said, "No rush. They've always got hamsters in stock."

'"Yes," says Mum, "but any old hamster won't do, will it? We'll have to get one that looks like Cedric." Now, I hadn't thought of that. I mean, Cedric was a bit past it, but you could still see that he must have been quite impressive in his prime—about six months ago. They go off quickly. You couldn't pass off just any old short-back-and-sides hamster as Cedric. He was deep pile one hundred per cent natural fibres, Cedric was.'

'Most of them are,' Maurice observed. 'The day of the acrylic rodent has not dawned.'

'Around eleven o'clock I was thinking about bed because there didn't seem to be any more sex and violence on the box, and Mum says, "Hang about; make sure little Whatsisname's still in the land of the living," and I said, "Why don't you do it?" and she said, "You know what I'm like with dead animals," and I did. When poor old Ginger went to meet his maker she waited all day for one of us to come home and take him out of the laundry basket. He'd stiffened up and got wedged. It took ages to ma- noeuvre him out. Well, we opened up the cage and I moved the wood wool and there was Cedric— gone.'

'Gone where?'

'Gone where all good hamsters go, I imagine,' said Nazzer. 'To that Great Wheel in the sky. And he was on his back with his little feet in the air and his mouth open like he'd died taking a last nibble at something.

"Omygawd," says Mum, thinking of Mark. "Is he stiff yet?"

'So I poked him,' Nazzer said, 'and he . . . yielded.'

'It's a fair cop, Guv?'

'No, I mean he was still *elastic*. Mum said, "Curl him up. Make him look natural." I said, "He looks pretty natural to me. You can't get much more natural than dead," and she said, "Make him look like he's asleep and cover him over again," so I sort of re-arranged him with his paws over his little nose and then we made a big heap of wood wool and fluff with just a little bit of him showing at the back. Then we put a tea towel over his cage—sort of respect for the dead.

'"Right," says Mum, thinking at the speed of light. "I'll take Mark out tomorrow, first thing, and you can take Cedric and find a duplicate."

'"Mother," I said, or words to that effect, "I am not going to spend Saturday pedalling round Norwich with a dead hamster in my pocket."

'"You take him with you," Mum says, adamant like, "and find an exact match. You know how observant Mark is."'

'He's still observant,' Nina remarked. 'Last time I saw him he was in the bushes in Chapelfield Gardens with a pair of binoculars.'

'He's a growing lad,' Nazzer said, tolerantly. 'Anyway, we were all so busy trying to shield him from death that we forgot to shield him from sex as well.

'Next morning up he gets and goes galloping down to visit Cedders—but I was there before him. I said, "Hang on, Mark. Don't disturb him. We gave him a drop of brandy last night to strengthen his little heart, and he's still sleeping it off.''

'"But I want to see him," says Mark, a bit tearful, so I took the pall—the tea towel—off the cage, and there was the pile of wood wool and a little glimpse of Cedric down the hole—moving!'

'Had you really given him brandy?' Nina said. 'D'you mean he was only stoned?'

'I think that's disgusting,' Maurice said, 'corrupting small and furries.'

'He was *not* stoned,' Nazzer said. 'What Mark didn't know was that I'd rigged Cedric up on the fish slice with the handle poking out at the back of the cage, under the tea towel. While Mark was mooing and drooling and making little furry noises at the front, I was moving the handle up and down at the back. It looked quite convincing, though I do say it myself,' Nazzer said, modestly.

'You really went to all that trouble so he wouldn't know the hamster had snuffed it?'

'Wasn't my idea,' Nazzer said. 'When I have a son and the hamster hangs up his skates, I'll dissect it on the breadboard so he'll know the meaning of life. Anyway, Mark says goodbye to Cedric and Mum took him out for a nice bus ride to Ipswich or somewhere like that—really foreign and exciting, and I put Cedric in a paper bag and cycled across to Dereham Road.

'The guy in the pet shop looked quite pleased to have a customer until I took Cedric out of the bag, then he sort of *reeled* and clutched his forehead and yelled "No! Not another one!"

'"You got a run on dead hamsters?" I said.

'He said, "Whaddya mean, dead? I thought you were trying to sell it." I said, "Is there a market for them, then?" I mean, it hadn't occurred to me that anyone might want to buy Cedric, not in his condition,' Nazzer said. 'And the guy says, "No, but I've had it up to here with buying back baby guinea-pigs. I thought your friend there was a guinea-pig." I felt almost proud of old Cedders—I mean, he was pretty big for a hamster—though I'd been thinking he looked more like a rat that'd had a tail job. So anyway, I explained I needed a replacement, one that would match. The pet shop guy shows me his stock. Dozens of them, lying about in heaps but all very small. Did you know that baby hamsters sleep in heaps?'

'It's called clumping,' Maurice said. 'I don't know where I read that. It's amazing how the mind retains useful information, isn't it?'

'That's useful?' Nina said. 'See how useful it feels when you come to your Biology re-sit. Question: describe, with diagrams, the gastric system of the natterjack toad. Answer: I don't know anything about anybody's gastric system because someone tore the page out, but baby hamsters sleep in clumps.'

'*I* was getting an attack of the small and furries by this time,' Nazzer said. 'They are quite sweet, little hamsters. And all those baby mice like white bumble-bees on stalks. But I said, "Haven't you got anything bigger?" and the pet shop guy says, "Well there's not a lot of call for big ones. You can see what happens to them when they get big," and he pointed to Cedric. "Why do you want it, just as a matter of interest?" I explained about Mark's half-term and the guy says,

"You'd be surprised how often that happens. Take a small one, the kiddy won't notice." "Better not," I said. "Old Cedric here is a bit striking," and he had to agree. "Your best bet," he says, "is to go round your mates and see if anybody's got one the same size." I had this horrible vision of all of us with little brothers and sisters rushing round Norwich over half-term trying to swap hamsters with each other. I put Cedric back in his bag and went off to Ber Street, then the Castle pet shop. It was rodents, rodents, all the way,' Nazzer said. 'Gerbils, hamsters, mice, rats, guinea-pigs, chipmunks. Just about everything except coypu and capybaras.'

'You'd have to go to the Broads for a coypu,' Nina said. 'You ever *seen* a coypu? They've got orange teeth—like slices of carrot.'

'They used to be farmed for their fur,' Maurice said.

'Pull the other one.'

'Yes they were. It was called Nutria, but they broke out of the farms and headed for the Broads.'

'Just like Brummies,' Nina said. 'The Broads are full of Brummies in summer. I'd as soon wear a wet hearth rug, myself. Than a coypu, that is.'

'Dare say the coypu would support that,' Nazzer said. 'I don't suppose coypu regard it as the summit of achievement to end up round somebody's neck. Cedric would have made a good fur coat. You'd have needed a lot of him, though.'

'You'd think with genetic engineering that they'd have managed to breed coat-sized hamsters by now, wouldn't you?' Maurice said. 'I mean, they can cross sheep with goats.'

'You'd have to cross a hamster with a cow,' Nazzer said.

Nina said, 'What do you get if you cross a camel with a dentist?'

'Dunno. What?'

'A hump-backed bridge.'

'I don't get that,' Maurice said.

'*Anyway*,' Nazzer said, 'I did every bleeding pet shop in Norwich. No Cedric look-alikes. So I thought about what the pet shop guy had said. I was having coffee in Stompers at the time and I suddenly saw Cardy Owen across the bar and I remembered that Naomi Harris was her best mate—'

'Not any more,' Nina said. 'They haven't spoken to each other since that disco at the end of the fifth year—'

'This was in the old days,' Nazzer said. 'Naomi lived up Unthank Road, then, and I knew they had hamsters. They used to breed them. So I rushed out and leapt on my bike. I was half-way up St Stephen's before I remembered Cedric. I'd left him on the table in his paper bag. So I did this U-turn and went boring back again. You know what it's like in Stompers— they only clear the tables twice a day. He was still there—'

'I geddit!' Maurice said. 'Dentures.'

'What did you want him back for?' Nina said. 'A keepsake?'

'Well, I knew that if I didn't get a replacement I'd have to make with the fish slice again. I rushed in and the paper bag was still on the table where I'd left it, but there were all these bikers sitting round it, real hairy heavies with *NECROPHILIACS DIE FOR IT* stencilled on their jackets. I got worried then. People like that *eat* hamsters. So I thought, Well, it's no good asking nicely, they won't know what the words mean, so I just dashed in, grabbed the bag and shot out again. And they all came roaring out after me—that should have tipped me off something was wrong—but I was on my bike—call me Tebbit—and off up the road again. So anyway, I went round to Naomi's and she was in. I said, "Look, do us a favour. I want to borrow a hamster," and she says, "What for?" I said, "Just a substitution job. Ours has turned up his toes." "Can't you buy a new one?" she says. "Not like I want," I said, and I explained what had happened and how Cedric was kind of unusual. So she turns to this wall of hamster modules and says, "OK. I'll try and match you up with one of our old ones. Let's have a look at him." So I opened the bag,' Nazzer said, 'and she said, "Is this some kind of a joke, Pollard?" It wasn't Cedric in the bag. It was a quarter-pound Stomperburger with onions and cheese.'

'You mean—the bikers had got Cedric?'

'Well, if they had, they probably *had* eaten him,' Nazzer said. 'I didn't feel much like going back to find out. I wondered if they'd noticed. Poor old Cedders. Naomi was creased up, rolling about on the floor and kicking the furniture. She actually *gave* me a hamster in the end. It was huge. Just like Cedric except in one important detail—only I didn't spot it at the time. And I wanted to get away before Naomi had hysterics. The rest of the family was starting to join in and I had to get home before Mum and Mark did.'

'You got away with it then?' Nina said.

'Up to a point,' Nazzer said. 'Only I didn't quite find out why Naomi was screaming until the end of the week and Cedric Mark Two had kittens.'

'Kittens?'

'Pups, calves, cubs . . . whatever it is hamsters give birth to. That was why she was so huge. They only come into season for about thirty seconds every six months, or something like that, so it was a chance in a million. Mark was happy, though. "Is that why Cedric wasn't feeling well?" he kept saying. We had to say yes.'

'Must have given him some odd ideas about the facts of life, though,' said Maurice. 'No wonder he hangs about with binoculars in Chapelfield Gardens. He must be dead worried by now in case it happens to him.'

6

Light-Sensitive

'Well, would you?' Maurice said. 'If you had to *define* me, would you call me a poetical type?'

'Frankly, no,' Nazzer said. 'Neanderthal, yes. Adenoidal, possibly; not poetical. It was the poetry did for you in English Lit.'

'It was Lisa Pestell did for him in Eng. Lit.,' Nina said. 'Anyway, Neanderthals died out. I remember doing Neanderthals at the Middle School. They all suffered from arthritis very badly. Cro-Magnon Man had a walkover.'

'I've always thought that that was a very suspect theory,' Nazzer observed. 'I believe it's based on wishful thinking. Look at it this way, modern man is supposed to be descended from the Cro-Magnons, but it stands to reason, doesn't it, we'd want to kid ourselves that's where we came from—tall, upright, handsome, high-forehead, plenty of chin—'

'Chins are important,' Maurice said. 'Look at the Royal Family. They don't have a lot in the mandible department. Every now and then one of them gets sent out to marry a chin.'

'Exactly; we don't like to think we've come down from a bunch of low-brows with no chins at all, but there are plenty of people around who are dead ringers for Neanderthal Man. Look at the Witchards—*all* the Witchards. Look at Langham.'

'I think Langham goes back further than Neanderthal Man,' Nina said. 'Langham's ancestors had opposable toes.'

Maurice said, 'Neanderthal Man has had a bad press. There's a lot of evidence now to suggest that he had a heavier brain than us. His chin was just a sort of recessive characteristic.'

'Of course,' Nazzer said, 'the Hapsburgs had the problem in reverse. Too much chin.'

'You'd think they could have come to some arrangement with our lot,' Maurice said. 'Sort of cancelled each other out.'

'Neanderthal Man's due for a revival,' Nazzer said. 'Some good PR and a press agent and he'll be rehabilitated in no time. Quite a lot of the ground work's been done already. First of all it turns out that Neanderthal Man had a pretty impressive brain after all, not just a damp rubbery blob like we've been led to suppose. Next thing we know, someone'll prove that he was tall and handsome all along, it's just that his skeleton didn't keep very well, *then* it'll turn out that he invented gunpowder and movable type. Hey presto! The stage will be set. Suddenly it will be perfectly respectable to be descended from Neanderthal Man.'

'Good news for you, then,' Nina said, to Maurice.

'What's all this with the Neanderthals anyway?' Maurice demanded. 'I only asked if you thought I was a poetical type.'

'Baskerville type,' Nazzer mused. 'Howling in the

night, the Great Grimpen Mire, the game's afoot, Watson.'

'What's all this with the poetry?' Nina said. 'Are we supposed to compare thee with a summer's day?'

'What, him?' Nazzer said. 'A summer's day? How about a winter's night?'

'Or a fall of soot? Or a pound of mince,' Nina said. 'Or a garden gnome.'

'Shall I compare thee to a garden gnome? Brilliant, Write it down.'

'Thou are more lovely . . . what comes next?' Nina said, scribbling on the formica table top.

'Not that bit. How can you be as lovely as a garden gnome? Think of the average garden gnome; bow legs, pointed head, looks stoned out of its mind.'

'This isn't still meant to be *me*, is it?' Maurice said. 'Why not compare me to a rubber plant, while you're at it?'

'Shall I compare thee to a rubber plant? You're thin and spindly and you're turning brown . . . That'll do. Write it down, Nina.'

'People always think that long words are poetical,' Maurice said, 'but when it comes down to actually doing it, it's the little short ones that are easiest to handle.'

'That's true of most little short things,' Nazzer said.

'People who try to write poetry always use words with about seven syllables that don't rhyme with anything,' Nina said.

'Not many words rhyme with *anything*; penny swing . . . Jenny King—hey, d'you remember Jenny

King? In the third year? I wonder what happened to her,' Maurice said.

'Shakespeare didn't,' Nazzer said. 'Shakespeare stuck to short ones, mainly. That's probably how he managed to write so much. He didn't have to sit around for hours looking through Roget's *Thesaurus*.'

'It's amazing how complicated he managed to make them,' Maurice said. 'Still, I suppose it must take a genius to be confusing with words like "and" and "but". You'd think someone tipped him off he was going to end up on an O level paper. Make 'em sweat, Bill.'

'Yes, but he *wasn't* writing for O level candidates, was he?' Nazzer said. 'He was writing for soccer hooligans.'

'They didn't have soccer in those days,' Nina said, 'just the bladder. There weren't any rules or a league or anything. They used to play it in the street and people got killed—playing, that is, not watching.'

'Yes, but the sort of people who watched his plays would be soccer hooligans if they were around today. Where was his theatre—Southwark. That's probably Millwall territory now. I bet Shakespeare's audiences were the ancestors of the South Bank Slashers or whatever. At the end of the play they'd invade the pitch—the stage. I don't suppose they went to *watch Hamlet*, just to riot in the middle of Act Four.'

'He's right,' Maurice said. 'We read *The Merchant of Venice* in the fifth year. There's someone in that called Gobbo. You can just imagine him down Carrow Road with a spray can: *Gobbo woz ere*.'

'A summer's day is lovely but thou aren't . . .'

'That's good,' Nazzer said. 'That scans. Keep going, write it down.'

'You haven't got that down about me being thin and spindly and turning brown, have you? I can't be thin and spindly *and* Neanderthal.'

'Poetic licence,' Nina said. 'And you are turning brown. You always do in June. It's sickening, the colour you go without even trying. People lie on the beach and get sunstroke, trying to look like you. People buy sun beds.'

'There's no plumbing the depths of human idiocy,' Nazzer said.

Maurice said, 'Trees can get sunburn.'

'Pull the other one.'

'I read this article. Trees with smooth bark, like beeches, overheat. The ones with fissured bark stay cool. Silver birches reflect.'

'Us reflective types don't tan easily,' Nazzer said. 'That's indisputable. And you can't get much more fissured than old Patterson—look at *him*. Stays the colour of a dead fish all summer.'

'It must be Maurice's smooth bark makes him so attractive,' Nina said.

'I don't get sunstroke,' said Maurice.

'How do you keep a tree out of the sun?' Nazzer asked. 'It would grow incredibly thin and tall, like rhubarb.'

'Like telegraph poles,' Nina muttered. 'That's the whole point of keeping a tree out of the sun.'

'I only asked—' Maurice began.

'Asked what?'

'If you thought I was—oh, never mind. I just

thought you might have noticed I hadn't been around much, lately.'

'Lately? Look,' Nazzer said, patiently, 'what makes you think we'd notice if you weren't around? You're *never* around. That's what you're famous for.'

'It's so time consuming,' Nina said. 'You think of all the hours you spend explaining why you didn't turn up; it'd be quicker *to* turn up. Then you could spend the time you spend explaining why you didn't turn up doing whatever it was you would have been doing if you *had* turned up.'

'I don't follow that,' Maurice said, after a pause.

'You didn't do all that well in the language paper either, come to think of it,' Nazzer mused.

'All I meant was, I thought you might have thought I'd been a bit preoccupied this last week or so.'

'There's skirt in this, somewhere,' Nina murmured.

'Watch your lip,' Maurice said. 'This was no skirt, this was a lady. Only I didn't realize it was a lady to start with.'

'A transvestite?' Nazzer suggested.

'Funny, isn't it?' Nina said. 'A bloke wearing a dress is in drag, but a woman wearing trousers is just a woman wearing trousers.'

'*Just* a woman wearing trousers? There was a long hard battle fought so that people like you could wear trousers,' Nazzer said. 'Long before suffragettes were chaining themselves to railings, Mrs Arabella Bloomer was wearing harem pants.'

'Suffragettes weren't demonstrating for the right to wear trousers.'

'I was in the bus station,' Maurice said.

'Where were you *meant* to be?'

'Right there, smart-arse,' Maurice said. 'It was Saturday. I was waiting for the bus home only I wasn't—'

'Why weren't you catching the train?'

'I'd arranged to meet someone on the bus,' Maurice said, 'only there was someone I *didn't* want to meet at the bus stop.'

'Who?' Nina said.

'You remember that girl—no, it doesn't matter.'

'Aye-aye,' Nazzer said. 'Which girl is this? No, let me guess. Not—Warty Samantha Nudd from Neatishead?'

'That was years ago,' Nina said. 'Warty Samantha's been going with Gareth for yonks. And she hasn't got warts any more. She had them charmed.'

'You'd think someone with A level Biology could do better than wart charming,' Nazzer said.

'It's sympathetic magic,' Nina said, 'like rain dancing.'

'Wart dancing,' Nazzer said, thoughtfully. 'It sounds like some kind of ancient folk festival, based on a prehistoric fertility rite, naturally, like the Helston Floral Dance.'

'The Neatishead Wart Dance. You can imagine them gambolling up and down the street with flowers round their hats and bells on their knees and everybody's pissed by lunchtime. There's nothing like that in Norfolk. We could do with a wart dance—a tourist attraction.'

'Some of us don't need an excuse to get pissed by lunchtime,' Nina said.

'It was *not* Warty Samantha.'

'Who, the one you wanted to meet or the one you didn't want to meet?'

'Either of them,' Maurice said. 'The point is, I went and stood down the other end of the bus station, next to the photography booth—you know, where you can get a mug shot for your passport before you leap on the bus for Kathmandu via Bury St Edmunds. Anyway, there was someone in it. Those silly green curtains that only come half-way down—'

'I wonder why they only come half-way down,' Nina said.

'In the interests of public decency,' Nazzer suggested. 'If they came all the way down people might go inside and do naughty things. On *film*.'

'If you were so desperate for it you'd use a photo booth I shouldn't think you'd stop to worry about drawing the curtains,' Maurice said. 'Look what happens in phone boxes. Well, these little curtains were drawn and I could see these legs—'

'Oh god, legs again. I knew there was skirt in it somewhere.'

'You know what I think,' Maurice said. 'I think you're a female chauvinist pig.'

'That's rich,' Nina said. 'That's rich coming from you.'

'It doesn't sound right—women talking about skirt,' Maurice said.

'Female chauvinist sow,' Nazzer amended.

'Skirt isn't women,' Nina said. 'It's a technical term. Skirt's what holds up the action in thrillers.'

'This is a thriller, is it?' Nazzer said. 'Personally, I haven't been so excited since we joined the EEC.'

'Like Lois Lane,' Nina said. 'She's only there to be rescued.'

'You know what it's like in those booths,' Maurice said. 'You sit there feeling a total prat because you know people can see your legs.'

'You have a leg fetish,' Nazzer remarked.

Nina said, 'Yeah, like in those public loos where the door starts half-way up the wall.'

'We don't have that problem,' Nazzer said.

'Well, suddenly,' Maurice said, 'there was this squawk from inside the booth and the curtains flew open and this woman rushed out—nearly knocked me flat—'

'Oh-ho, a big one.'

'Well, I'd just been standing there, looking at her knees. I didn't notice that the lights had changed, if you see what I mean. And she rushed off—you know how crowded it gets round the bottom end of the bus station, outside the buffet. I couldn't see where she went, but a few minutes later one of the double-deckers pulled out. I think it was the one that goes through Acle.'

'Why didn't you go and look?' Nina said. 'Why didn't you go and leap on it? I'd've thought that was more your style. I mean you went to Haddiscoe after skirt. You went to *Thetford* once.'

'Because of the photos,' Maurice said. 'It takes about four minutes to get them developed in those machines, and she'd left them behind.'

'It usually looks more as if it took four seconds,' Nazzer said, 'and you come out like something that was lurking behind a mosquito net in dense fog.'

'I wanted to see what she looked like—so I'd recognize her again. I mean, I kind of got a glimpse, but I wasn't looking at her face when she came rushing out. So I hung about, and after a bit the photos arrived. They were worth waiting for,' Maurice said. 'It was definitely a woman, though.'

'What were you expecting?' Nazzer asked. 'No, don't bother to answer that. You're getting very odd in your old age, Nicholls. Legs . . . trees . . .'

'It wasn't a *girl*, I mean,' Maurice said. 'It was a woman.'

'I can't actually see you as anybody's toyboy,' Nina said.

'She really was a looker,' Maurice said. 'It was hot that day, really hot, and she was wearing a straw hat and a frock with a sort of scooped-out top, very low.'

'You mean, you didn't notice *that*?' Nazzer said, scandalized.

'Yes I did. I'm telling you—'

'I meant when she rushed out of the booth, fleshly and *quivering*—'

'He was leg-watching.'

'She had a silk begonia in her hat, well, something like, and she'd done four different poses for the photographs. One looking straight ahead, and two sort of glancing sideways only one was smudged a bit where she'd moved too soon, but the fourth was terrific. She had her head bent and she was looking up through her eyelashes. It wasn't the sort of thing you could use in a passport, though. The frontier patrols would think they were being bribed, or something.'

'Half the time no one looks at your passport,' Nina

said. 'They don't even stamp it, half the time. Most people don't look like their passport photographs anyway. I look mad in mine.'

'Evidently a poor likeness.'

'I look dead in mine,' Nazzer said. 'I look embalmed, a kind of unearthly pallor.'

'You could have it put on your gravestone,' Nina said, 'like the Italians do.'

'They dig you up again in Naples,' Maurice said. 'After two years, they dig you up again and dust you off. It's a kind of spring cleaning, I suppose.'

'It's a good idea, photographs on gravestones,' Nina said. 'It's a pity we don't have them here, it wouldn't half liven up the churchyards. I think it's terrible the way everybody has to have the same thing, these days. You never get angels and urns, any more. They don't even come to a point, any more.'

. 'The angels?'

'It's on account of good taste,' Maurice said. 'Death's got to be tasteful these days. When you go into a graveyard you aren't meant to think Cor! I'm going to die too, you think, Ow, don't they keep it nice?'

'The Government ought to deregulate tombstones,' Nazzer said, 'the way they did the buses. I think that could be a really popular move. A return to Victorian values, urns, angels, skulls—'

'And lies,' Nina said. 'You get really good lies on old tombstones. They were a sort of early version of the Deaths column in the EDP. *Sadly missed . . . suddenly taken . . . one of these days we will understand . . .* and you know all time this guy was an evil old toad who knocked his wife about and quarrelled with the neighbours.'

'Well,' Maurice said, 'I was wondering what to do with these pictures.'

'Why didn't you wear them next to your heart as a memory of what might have been?'

'You ever tried wearing a photograph next to your heart?' Maurice demanded. 'It goes all soft and sticks to your nipple.'

'Unlike most people,' Nazzer remarked, 'you're in a position to know.'

'I was wondering how to get them back to her. I mean, there was a chance she was a tourist, just passing through, but the way she went after that bus it looked like she knew where she was going. Then I thought perhaps she caught it every day, and if I went back—'

'Don't tell me,' Nazzer cried, 'this is your dark secret. You've been down the bus station every day, searching for her. Dangling around the photo booth looking wistful, in a paleolithic way.'

'You haven't, have you?' Nina said. '*Every day?*'

'A bit,' Maurice admitted. 'Just between four o'clock and the Acle bus pulling out.'

'I think that *is* poetical,' Nina said. 'Don't you, Naz?'

'No I don't,' Nazzer said. 'I think there's a musical in it; *The Phantom of the Bus Station*. There's this hideously mutilated schoolboy, see, with a strip of photographs in his pocket that nobody wants to look at. Once upon a time he was hanging out of a window in Magdalene Street when a bus went by too close and made a nasty mess of his head as he was craning his neck to take a snap of the fair unknown—'

'Unknown what?'

'Knees,' Nina said.

'Ever since, he's worn a false head and haunts the bus station, swinging athletically from bus to bus and finally dropping on to someone's head from the top of the Norwich Union. Music by Andrew Lloyd Webber, book and lyrics by A. J. Pollard. It will run and run.'

'It will drip and trickle.'

'Well, I did go back,' Maurice said. 'Every day till yesterday.'

'Yesterday was crunch time, eh?' said Nazzer. 'Yesterday was moment-of-truth day.'

'Did she show up again?' Nina said. 'You found her?'

'I had the pictures to go on,' Maurice said. 'It was a good thing really that she was so unusual-looking. If she'd just been normal—'

'In what way was she abnormal?' Nazzer inquired. 'Take your time answering that one—and don't write on both sides of the paper at once.'

'*If*,' Maurice went on, 'she had been ordinary it might have been harder to pick her out. It could have been dead embarrassing. Imagine it, going up to a strange woman with a photograph and saying, "Excuse me, madam, is this you?" They might take it as an insult.'

'Good way of getting yourself arrested.'

'This one, though, you couldn't mistake her. As soon as I saw her coming up from Surrey Street I knew who it was.'

'Kind of radiant, was she?'

'She was wearing the same dress, though she didn't have the hat on,' Maurice said. 'And then there were the legs—'

'Ah yes, the legs. *Les jambes* as they say in France. Legs sounds sexier though, doesn't it?'

'No,' Nina said, 'it doesn't. You're just thinking of the concept of legs. Legs isn't much of a word as words go.'

'Like *Romeo and Juliet*, you mean? *What's in a name? That which we call a rose by any other name would smell as sweet* . . . You mean, if we called it a leg it would still smell sweet?'

'Oh yerse,' Nina said. 'Imagine some geezer coming home from work with a bouquet for his wife: "Oh darling, what a lovely bunch of legs." '

'Tell you what,' Nazzer said, 'this explains his unwholesome fascination with trees. Legs remind him of young saplings.'

'She was going at a hell of a lick, but the bus wasn't due to leave for another ten minutes and on past form she seemed to be turbo-charged anyway. And she came up level with the photo booth—look, you must think I'm bonkers. I'd had this idea all the time that she'd come back for another go of pictures—on account of having lost the first lot. It hadn't struck me that she could have had another go somewhere else. You get those booths all over the place, now. Anyway, I was a bit surprised when she didn't slow down so I sort of leapt out—'

'You *are* going to get arrested, one of these days.'

'If you're going to start jumping on strange

women,' Nazzer advised, 'you should go up on Mousehold. More cover,' he added.

'I said, "Excuse me, I think these are yours." And she stopped and looked at me like I was trying to blackmail her. So I whipped out the photos—'

'She must have been *sure* you were trying to blackmail her.'

'—and I said, "You left these behind last week. I recognized you."

'And she smiled at me. It was a really terrific smile,' Maurice said, 'only, of course, now that I was getting a good look at her, I could see that she really was—wasn't—I mean, much—not so—'

'An Older Woman?' Nazzer suggested.

'Well . . .'

'An *Old* Woman?'

'Nah, not an *old* woman. Older, yes, but she wasn't grey or anything.'

'Amazing what you can get out of a bottle these days,' Nina murmured, scribbling again.

'*Or* lined. It wasn't dyed, Nina. She didn't look anything like as old as she must be—but she looked a lot older than the photographs. And she gave me this smile, and she said, "Have you been keeping them for me? How sweet." And I just stood there like an idiot.'

'Looking sweet.'

'And I was just beginning to wonder if she realized that I'd been hanging about for her. And wondering if I *wanted* her to realize. Some people you'd want to know you were looking for them, but it wasn't her I fancied, just her knees. And she wasn't quite what I was expecting.'

'Grandmotherly?'

'Worse than that. I was sort of mumbling about thinking they might have been important when this voice behind me says, "Come on, Mum, we'll miss the bus again." I *knew* that voice,' Maurice said, 'and I looked round and there was Langham.'

'*Langham*? Our Langham?'

'Him, yes. She says, "Oh, there you are, pet." '

'Langham's got a *mother*?'

'They weren't winding you up, were they?' Nina said.

'I always thought he was grown in a Petri dish,' Nazzer said, 'from cells.'

'Come off it,' Maurice said. 'Only Langham's mother could call Langham "pet". And Langham stood there, with his shoulders round his ears and his knuckles sweeping the ground, making out that Neanderthal Man was an advanced life form compared to him, and he makes this noise in his chest—round about where his larynx is—'

'Sort of level with his armpits?'

'More or less. Any lower and you'd just think his stomach was rumbling. And giving me very funny looks. And his mum says, "Thanks for keeping my pictures safe." They went off after the bus. She doesn't look wild enough to be Langham's mother. I've been avoiding Langham all day.'

'He's not adopted, is he?'

'No, his sisters are the same shape. They must take after their old man. Mum—Mrs Langham's got a neck,' Maurice said.

'And knees,' Nina said.

'You ought to lay off women,' Nazzer advised. 'Stick to trees.'

'Hey, look,' Nina said, pointing to the table top. 'We've written a sonnet.'

Shall I compare thee to a rubber plant?
You're thin and spindly and you're turning brown.
A summer's day is lovely, but thou aren't.
That's good, that scans, keep going, write it down.
Trees can get sunburn. Pull the other one.
Trees with smooth bark like beeches overheat.
How do you keep a tree out of the sun?
Imagine them gambolling up and down the street.
This woman rushed out, nearly knocked me flat,
She really was a looker. It was hot.
She had a silk begonia in her hat,
And I just stood there like an idiot.
        It wasn't her I fancied, just her knees.
        You ought to lay off women. Stick to trees.

7

'And now, these hot days, is the mad blood stirring'

'If you ask me,' Nina said, 'it wouldn't have happened at all if Nidsworth hadn't turned up with those two Japanese radishes.'

'Nidsworth,' Nazzer said, 'is your genuine, five-star, gold-plated, lead-lined, card-carrying nutter.'

'Not such a nutter as Catton,' said Maurice. 'Remember him? He had tattoos all over his head.'

'I thought that was pretty far-sighted of him, actually,' Nazzer said. 'Unlike your average yob he knew he wasn't always going to be a Ber Street Boot Boy or whatever his outfit called themselves. The others had strip cartoons practically, up to the shoulders; indelible. When Catton becomes an adult —or if—all he'll have to do is let his hair grow to conceal his origins. No one will guess that he used to be an anthropoid Nazi when he was seventeen.'

'Huh, wait till he's seventy,' Nina said. 'Wait till he goes bald from natural causes. He'll look pretty daft queuing up for his pension with a skull and dripping dagger on his bonce.'

'It won't look so bad as tattooed arms,' Maurice said. 'At least there's some surface tension on your head, but the arms, I mean, tattooed *flab*. What happens to a tattoo when it gets wrinkled? What'll it look like?'

'Do you remember pound notes?' Nazzer said.

'God, that makes me feel old,' Maurice said. 'The fivers will be the next to go. We'll be able to tell our grandchildren, Ah, I can remember when money was made of paper.'

'By the time we've got grandchildren,' Nina said, 'money will be made of plastic. You'll have to go to a museum to see coins.'

'Anyway,' Nazzer said, 'remember what pound notes looked like after you'd left them in your pocket and Mum put your trousers in the washing machine?'

'Yes,' said Maurice.

'That's what a wrinkled tattoo will look like.'

'Nidsworth isn't tattooed,' Nina said. 'He doesn't even wear an ear-ring. Nidsworth wears a suit and a bowler hat on Saturdays and rides round in taxis. Haven't you seen him? He sits bolt upright in the back with a rolled umbrella and the *Financial Times*, playing at city gents.'

'I only see him at school,' Maurice said. 'We don't have anything like Nidsworth out at Worstead. It's different out in the sticks. We don't have duels out there.'

'We don't have all that many in Norwich,' Nazzer said.

'It wasn't meant to be a duel anyway,' Nina said. 'It was meant to be a punch-up; gouging, nutting and boot-in-the-groin stuff. When that fellow started mauling Lisa Pestell—'

'Lisa Pestell?' Maurice said. 'I didn't know she was involved. Is she all right?'

'Calm down,' Nina said. 'She just happened to be bopping with Nidsworth—'

'But she said she'd decided to stay in and revise.'

'She did revise,' Nazzer said. 'She revised her decision. That's why she was at the disco. Sorry, Maurice.'

'Anyway,' Nina said, 'this Geordie guy grabbed her—quite politely, I mean, it wasn't about to be rape or anything like that—and Nidsworth says, "Sir, you are handling the woman I love." '

'Oh Jesus.' Maurice put his head down on the table.

'Cool it, brother,' Nazzer said. 'That was only Nidsworthspeak for Get your dirty mitts off my girl.'

'She's not his girl—is she?'

'Someone wrote *Wayne Grey 4 Lisa Pestell* in the ladies' bog at Stompers,' Nina said, 'but that was just to get at Naomi Harris. Nay's been going with Wayne for centuries. It doesn't mean anything.'

'Wayne's been eyeing her, though,' Maurice said.

'Anyway, this Geordie turns round and he gets a look at Nidsworth for the first time, a *proper* look, I mean. Up till then it had just been some loony in black, jumping up and down.'

'Nidsworth doesn't *look* barmy, though,' Maurice said. 'You wouldn't be able to tell just from seeing him.'

'It was his clothes,' Nina said. 'He was wearing a tail

coat and a frilly shirt and a wing collar. And a velvet bow tie. Well, I don't think it was a bow tie, tell you the truth. I think it was a ladies' garter—you can get them from that shop that sells rude knickers in Magdalene Street. But the Geordie was expecting a punch in the teeth. He didn't think he was going to get flicked round the face with a kid glove.'

'He didn't, did he?'

'Who didn't what?'

'Nidsworth never flicked this geezer round the face with a kid glove?'

'He did. He whipped it out of his pocket like he kept it there especially for flicking people,' Nina said. 'The way some people carry Stanley knives; just in case.'

'I wonder who Stanley was,' Nazzer said.

'Stanley?'

'The guy who invented the knife. It's the wrong sort of name for a knife, really. Bowie knife, yes. Gatling gun, Stilson wrench—'

'Nissen hut?'

'—but *Stanley* knife . . . It hasn't got the right ring to it.'

'More like Bunsen burner,' Nina said. 'Bunsen could only be a scientist. You can just imagine him scrabbling about in a lab causing minor explosions. You couldn't be a racing driver or an astronaut with a name like Bunsen.'

'Same with Stanley,' Nazzer said. 'Little bloke in a brown overall, out in the garden shed carving plant-pot holders and pipe racks. And his old lady comes to the back door and yells, "Tea's ready, Stan," and in he comes dropping wood shavings all over the carpet.'

'What did the Geordie do?' Maurice asked, fretfully.

'He just stared for starters,' Nazzer said; 'then he made unintelligible Tyneside noises.'

'I *think* he said, "Do you want your teeth knocked out the back of your neck, you fairy ponce?"' Nina murmured, 'something like that, you know, provocative. And Nidsworth said, "Are you demanding satisfaction, Sir?" and the Geordie goes on growling about boots and teeth.'

'He was at a disadvantage, though,' Nazzer said, 'on account of he didn't have any mates with him. If he'd had back-up, air cover, I reckon we'd have been peeling Nidsworth off the floor like a squashed frog.'

'He looked all round him,' Nina said, 'and saw the rest of us closing in, sort of drawn there, like magnetism. Like at school, when there's a fight in the playground. Everybody knows, even before it starts. Nidsworth's still flapping his glove about and asking, ever so politely, "You *are* demanding satisfaction, aren't you, Mr . . . er . . ."'

'I don't think he'd ever been called *Mr* before,' Nazzer said. 'He seemed kind of bewildered, like someone had offered him a Masonic handshake and he didn't have enough fingers. I think he'd have got out of it if he could, but there was this solid wall of people round him and I expect his mother had warned him about savages in foreign parts.'

'No, I don't think that was it,' Nina said. 'I don't think anyone had *warned* him about Norwich. I think he'd been told we're all a load of soft worzels down in Norfolk, and there he was in the middle of the Monster Raving Loony Party.'

'That's a thought,' Maurice said. 'We should have got Nids to put up for the Monster Raving Loonies in the school election.'

'I'd wondered about that,' Nazzer said, 'me having got landed with the post of Returning Officer—by due democratic process, of course. *Right, Pollard, you be Returning Officer.* Nidsworth said he'd prefer to stand as SDP candidate, more his image, he said, but he didn't even vote in the end.'

'Provisional Wing of the SDP,' Nina said. 'Well, I suppose this Geordie—'

'What was his name?'

'I don't think we ever found out, did we, Naz? We just called him Geordie. He could see that if it wasn't a duel it would be a massacre, so he says "Ecky thump—"'

'That's Yorkshire,' Maurice said.

'What is?'

'They say Ecky thump in Yorkshire.'

'Ah,' Nazzer said. 'No wonder he was in such a snot. You might as well ask Boycott which side of the Medway he was born.'

'I bet he didn't say Ecky thump anyway. No one would actually *say* it.'

'It was hard to tell what he was saying,' Nina said. 'But in the end he sort of muttered, "OK. I demand satisfaction. I choose pistols." '

'You could see he wasn't entirely uneducated,' Nazzer said. 'He must have read the odd bodice-ripper.'

'What's a bodice-ripper?'

'Romance with heavy breathing,' Nazzer said. 'You

know, *the thin silk strained across her heaving bosom* . . . In your straight historical romance the thin silk just strains. In a bodice-ripper, it rips. Then he has his evil way with her.'

'Who does?'

'The villain.'

'Not in a bodice-ripper,' Nina said. 'In a bodice-ripper it's the hero who has his evil way. Anyway, people don't have bosoms in bodice-rippers. They have breasts.'

'And thighs,' Nazzer said. 'Not just—er—busts. You get a lot of thighs, too. And loins.'

'What the hell have you been reading, Naz?' said Maurice.

'I've never been sure what loins are, to be honest,' Nazzer admitted. 'I know you can get them in the butcher's, but where are they on *us*, that's what I ask myself.'

'Naughty bits.'

'I don't think so. When you ask for a loin of lamb in the butcher's you don't get naughty bits.'

'What the naughty bits are joined on to, then.'

'Isn't that groins?'

'Well, then,' Nina said, 'Nidsworth did one of his lightning changes into a normal human being. "Don't wind me up," he says. "Where are you going to find pistols in Norwich at eleven at night?"

'So Geordie says, "Who's winding who up?" but I think he cottoned on at that point that Nidsworth wasn't just mucking about. Well, of course he *was* mucking about, but he was serious with it. I mean, duelling with pistols was mucking about, because there weren't any pistols, but he wasn't fooling about the duel. "OK," says Geordie. "What do you suggest?" and Nidsworth says, "Moolies." '

'*What?*'

'Moolies—no, Geordie didn't know what they were, either, and nor did most of the others,' Nina said, 'but I did because I was there when he bought them. Geordie thought that Nids was being obscene and he sort of squared up, and Nids makes with the glove again, flic-flac. And he said, Nidsworth said, "Somebody go and get them, they're in the cloakroom." '

'What *are* moolies?' Maurice asked, plaintively.

'Like I was trying to tell you, these big Japanese radishes.'

'Duelling with radishes?'

'These aren't your normal English radish,' Nazzer said. 'You must have seen them, Maurice. They look like baby elephants' tusks. They're about thirty centimetres long.'

'These weren't,' Nina said. 'These were over forty centimetres. His mum—they're all nutters in that family—she'd asked him to get them in the market at lunchtime because they don't sell things like that down the corner shop, and she didn't need the stuff that night so he left them in the cloakroom when this disco turned up. They weren't likely to get nicked. Most people wouldn't have known what they were anyway. Wayne Grey went out to the cloakroom and fetched in this string bag. It wasn't just moolies. There was a couple of aubergines, and a sort of hairy lettuce—'

'Endive,' Nazzer said.

'—and kiwi fruit and an awful mauve thing that looked like a boiled foot with veruccas.'

'A yam,' said Nazzer. 'I believe Nidsworth's mum was planning an ethnic dinner party. There was a packet of vine leaves in there as well. When you consider what he could have picked as weapons, the Japanese radishes looked quite rational. They work out a lot cheaper than buying the ordinary little red round ones, too,' he added.

'I think he planned the whole thing,' Nina said. 'I think he wanted a chance to *do* something with those radishes.'

'They have that effect on you,' Nazzer admitted. 'As soon as you see a mooli you start wondering what you can do with it. No—right off you wonder what it's *meant* to be for; then you begin to speculate. The possibilities are endless. For one thing, it doesn't look much like food.'

'Wayne Grey says, "Look, don't start anything in here or they'll throw us out." It was a bit late to tell him not to start anything, I thought,' Nina said, 'but Nidsworth says, "Where then? We don't want to attract attention."'

'That's a laugh,' Maurice said, 'Nidsworth not wanting to attract attention.'

'He meant the rozzers,' Nina said. 'The Old Bill, the Fuzz, the Boys in Blue.'

'"What about seconds?" says Geordie. He was all clued up,' Nazzer said. 'He knew the ropes. He also knew he was a bit lacking in the seconds department, there only being one of him.'

'Wayne Grey says, "What about the kiwi fruit?" but

no one got the joke until about half an hour later,' Nina said. 'Nidsworth says to Wayne, "You be his second," and Wayne says, "I was going to be yours," and Nidsworth says, "Then consider yourself seconded. Never let it be said that I took advantage of a stranger. I'll have Gareth instead." Gareth's bigger than all three of them,' Nina said. 'If that wasn't taking advantage I don't know what is.'

'So anyway, we all went outside and Wayne says what about the car park? "If we go round behind the mini-buses," he says, "no one will see us from the street."'

'Nidsworth says, "I was thinking of the Ipswich Road roundabout—on the traffic island," but we managed to talk him out of that. There's usually a police car parked round the corner, waiting for trouble; specially at that time of night. He took it very badly though, didn't he, Naz?'

'He what?'

'Took it badly. He said the Law was cramping his style. He got very loud. "That's the trouble with England," he says. "We're supposed to love eccentrics but you try being eccentric on a low income," he says. "You try being eccentric on the dole and you end up before the Beak. Eccentric is spelt M-O-N-E-Y. Under thirty quid a week and it's spelt L-O-O-N-Y."'

'He should know,' Maurice said. 'Hey—he's not on the dole, is he?'

'He will be if he doesn't get his O levels this time round,' Nina said. 'Anyway, we persuaded him to go round the back of the mini-buses. It was the best place, really. You couldn't be seen from the road but it was quite light because of that street lamp half-way up the drive.

'"So what do you do now?" says Wayne Grey. "Stand back to back, walk twelve paces, turn and fire?" He was standing there holding the moolies in his arms like they were duelling pistols.'

'They were meant to be, weren't they?'

'Not under Nidsworth Rules. I think what Wayne and the Geordie had in mind was taking aim with the moolies and saying Bang-bang, but old Nidsworth was back on the reality kick. He says to the Geordie, "You choose first, Sir," so Geordie takes a radish and stood there looking a prize nit—didn't he, Naz?'

'Couldn't really see,' Nazzer mumbled. 'Standing at the back . . .'

'So Nidsworth takes the other one and starts weighing it up and tossing it about—real majorette stuff, and Wayne Grey says, "Look, Nids, you going to fight with it or eat it?" So Nidsworth gets serious again and says, "First to score three hits is the winner," and he springs back and draws his radish and yells, "On guard!" Everyone had got into a circle by then and somebody says, "Seconds out," so Gareth and Wayne got out of the way and Geordie says, "You finished pissing about?" and Nidsworth says "On guard!" again. He was dead elegant,' Nina said.

'It must be all that wrist-work he puts in with the *Financial Times* on Saturdays,' Maurice said.

'Oh, it was wrist-work all right. One arm over his head, sort of curving, and his knees bent, and the radish held out like a rapier. But the Geordie wasn't elegant, was he, Naz? He got his radish in two hands and made this terrific swipe sideways and grunted— bit like Jimmy Connors doing a base-line return. If he'd had a sword,' Nina said, 'he'd have had Nidsworth's head off. Everybody gasped, sort of, because suddenly it did look serious. Nidsworth hopped about a bit and made a few classy prods, but Geordie was really going mad, jumping around and swinging his radish, and then Nidsworth lunged forward and caught the Geordie under the arm with the point of his radish and Wayne Grey yells, "A hit!" Didn't he, Naz?'

'A very palpable hit.'

'He never said that.'

'That's what Osric says in *Hamlet*.'

'Wayne never said it. I mean, he hardly had a chance to say anything. The Geordie swung his radish and gave Nidsworth this mega-swipe over the ear and the top came off.'

'Off his ear?'

'Off the radish. But it was a hell of a whack. Nidsworth really reeled. He sort of staggered back into Gareth's arms—'

'He did need his second, then?'

'He didn't need Gareth. Gareth just chucked him back into the ring and the Geordie caught him another clout over the eye, this time, and Nidsworth says, ever so feeble, "I say, Sir. Desist. This is not cricket."'

'Well, it wasn't, was it?' Maurice said.

'Funny how cricket used to be a gentleman's game,' Nazzer said. 'Gentlemen and players. They all used to be so *slim*.'

'W. G. Grace wasn't slim. W. G. Grace came on like Giant Haystacks.'

'All right, but apart from him, I mean, compared with now. Look at Gatting. Look at Botham. We don't have a side, it's a wall. Looks like Stonehenge when we're fielding.'

'Geordie didn't think it was cricket, either. He said, "Ah so! Kendo warrior strike again," and in he comes for another wallop, only Wayne Grey dashes between them and yells "Time!"

'"Whose side are you on?" says Geordie, on account of Wayne being *his* second, but Wayne said they were doing three-minute rounds. Nidsworth was getting worried, you could see. You could see he didn't want to go into school next day all hacked about and have everybody know he'd been beaten up with a radish. And Geordie was leading, two to one. He only needed another hit. I don't think Nidsworth had planned it like that at all, do you, Naz?'

'Highly unlikely.'

'So Wayne yells, "Seconds out!" and they *sprang* together and hit each other smack on the radish, and Nidsworth's broke off about half-way down, and they just stood there, jabbing at each other with the handles.'

'Handles?'

'Well, the end bits.'

'Butts.'

'Yeah, the butts. They were better matched, now, because Geordie couldn't use his two-handed grip any more. Nids got the next hit right in Geordie's gut and

Gareth called time because I think Geordie was about to use his boots.

'Then Geordie sort of flourished his radish and said, "Prepare to die, White-eyes, tora tora tora," or something like, and Nidsworth says, "Hang on, where's the fair damsel?" and Geordie says "Yer what?" forgetting the Samurai bit, and Wayne says, "Her what you're fighting over. Where's she gone?"

'They didn't say anything for a bit. I think they'd forgotten that they were supposed to be fighting over Lisa, and we all looked round, but she'd gone. Did you notice her go, Naz?'

'No,' Nazzer said, pensively. 'No, I didn't notice.'

'"You mean she's took off?" says Geordie, and he really was *snarling* now and we all started peering about—you know how it is when you know you're not going to find something—looking behind the lamp post and under the mini-buses and that, and Geordie's muttering about what they do to girls like that who run off while two blokes are fighting over them back up in Kirkby—'

'Kirkby's in Lancashire,' Maurice observed.

'Wayne says, "How about fresh weapons?" and fetches out the aubergines, but Geordie had lost interest in duelling.'

'He *wasn't* a Geordie, you know,' Maurice insisted. 'Not from Kirkby. Didn't you see *A Letter to Breshznev*? That was Kirkby.'

'Well, he didn't come from anywhere south of Luton,' Nina said. 'He says to Nidsworth, "What would you have done if I'd won—and she'd still been here?"

124

'Nidsworth says, "My dear chap, I'd have given you my blessing." Geordie went very slitty-eyed at that. Maybe giving people your blessing means something different up north. "You got a knife?" he says.

'"No," says Nidsworth, "have you?"

'"Nah," says Geordie. "Is the bar still open?"

'"We could go round my brother's bedsit," says Gareth. "He had a party last night. He may have some left over." It was funny, wasn't it, Naz, the way people sort of separated when the beer was mentioned. All the fellows sort of drifted off in one direction . . . melted into the shadows, didn't they, Naz?'

'Melted . . . yeah,' Nazzer said.

'And where was Lisa?'

'I don't know,' Nina said. 'I haven't seen her since. I shouldn't worry, Maurice. It was only a couple of nights ago.'

'She can't have gone, as it were, far,' Nazzer said, preparing to leave.

'Hang about,' said Maurice. 'Hang on, a minute. Where were *you* while all this was going on?'

'Me?' Nazzer said. 'Where was *I*?'

'Yeah, where were *you*? You've been very quiet.'

'I am naturally taciturn,' Nazzer said. 'One doesn't have to do a Nidsworth in order to create an effect. Marmoreal calm's more my style—a kind of noble aloofness.'

'Noble in the chemical sense,' Maurice said. 'Inert. What were you up to while all this was going on with the radishes?'

'Didn't you stay, then?' Nina said. 'Didn't you see *any* of it?'

'Not after the first few minutes. Once you all went out to the mini-buses I more or less retired, not wishing to subscribe to a scene of gratuitous violence.'

Maurice was squinting hard. 'You never walked out on a fight in your life. Let's be having you. Where *did* you go?'

'Well,' Nazzer said modestly, examining his thumbnails, 'it was a dark night, you know. Muggers, rapists, werewolves . . . Someone had to see Lisa Pestell home.'

'You *what*?'

'Oh oh,' Nina said, 'here we go again. Moolies for two and coffee for one. Look, there isn't *room* for gratuitous violence in here—can't you go outside and do that? Nazzer! It may be the last day of term, but we've got to come back in September. Mind the table, Maurice. *Maurice!*'

Other great reads from **Red Fox**

Haunting fiction for older readers from Red Fox

THE XANADU MANUSCRIPT
John Rowe Townsend

There is nothing unusual about visitors in Cambridge.

So what is it about three tall strangers which fills John with a mixture of curiosity and unease? Not only are they strikingly handsome but, for apparently educated people, they are oddly surprised and excited by normal, everyday events. And, as John pursues them, their mystery only seems to deepen.

Set against a background of an old university town, this powerfully compelling story is both utterly fantastic and oddly convincing.

'An author from whom much is expected and received.' *Economist*

ISBN 0 09 9751801   £2.50

ONLOOKER   Roger Davenport

Peter has always enjoyed being in Culver Wood, and dismissed the tales of hauntings, witchcraft and superstitions associated with it. But when he starts having extraordinary visions that are somehow connected with the wood, and which become more real to him than his everyday life, he realizes that something is taking control of his mind in an inexplicable and frightening way.

Through his uneasy relationship with Isobel and her father, a Professor of Archaeology interested in excavating Culver Wood, Peter is led to the discovery of the wood's secret and his own terrifying part in it.

ISBN 0 09 9750708   £2.50

Other great reads from **Red Fox**

Enter the gripping world of the REDWALL saga

REDWALL   Brian Jacques

It is the start of the summer of the Late Rose. Redwall Abbey, the peaceful home of a community of mice, slumbers in the warmth of a summer afternoon. The mice are preparing for a great jubilee feast.

But not for long. Cluny is coming! The evil one-eyed rat warlord is advancing with his battle-scarred mob. And Cluny wants Redwall . . .

ISBN 0 09 951200 9   £3.50

MOSSFLOWER   Brian Jacques

One late autumn evening, Bella of Brockhall snuggled deep in her armchair and told a story . . .

This is the dramatic tale behind the bestselling *Redwall*. It is the gripping account of how Redwall Abbey was founded through the bravery of the legendary mouse Martin and his epic quest for Salmandastron. Once again, the forces of good and evil are at war in a stunning novel that will captivate readers of all ages.

ISBN 0 09 955400 3   £3.50

MATTIMEO   Brian Jacques

Slagar the fox is intent on revenge . . .

On bringing death and destruction to the inhabitants of Redwall Abbey, in particular to the fearless warrior mouse Matthias. Gathering his evil band around him, Slagar plots to strike at the heart of the Abbey. His cunning and cowardly plan is to steal the Redwall children—and Mattimeo, Matthias' son, is to be the biggest prize of all.

ISBN 0 09 967540 4   £3.50

'It's right on the edge of the marshes—'

'What is?'

'Reedham.'

'I know,' Nazzer said. 'My mum took me there for a picnic when I was a young lad. I fell in a dyke and nearly drowned.'

'Are you sure they got you out in time?' Nina said. 'Brain death can occur after four minutes. I mean, you might have got left under for five.'

'Brain *damage*, not brain death,' Nazzer said. 'Brain death's when they pull the plug on your life-support system and break you up for spares.'

'—at least,' Maurice went on, 'I thought it was like the end of the world until we got to Haddiscoe. There's *nothing* at Haddiscoe, just two platforms. There's not even a bridge or a subway—you have to walk across the lines.'